SPIRITS IN A MATERIAL WORLD

SPIRITS IN A MATERIAL WORLD

A Christmas Mystery

Colin Quashie

COLIN QUASHIE ART
www.quashie.com

Book layout & jacket design by Colin Quashie
Text set in 10-point Georgia

Registered: Writers Guild of America, West
Library of Congress Cataloging-in-Publication Data
is available for this book
ISBN 10: 0615281532
ISBN 13: 978-0-615-28153-7
This book may be purchased at:
www.createspace.com/3375879

To my everything; Cathy

In all the years I've dared to dream,
Never once did you try to wake me.

AUTHOR'S NOTE

Many of the names used in this book are those of family and very close friends. Their assignment to specific characters in no way implies any factual connection to fictional personalities. They are part and parcel and as such, inclusion in this endeavor is a humble way of recognizing and thanking them for their love and support over the years.

C. D. Q.

"...and what was light one instant, at another time was dark, so the figure fluctuated in its distinctness: being now a thing with one arm, now a pair of legs without a head, now a head without a body: of which dissolving parts, no outline would be visible in the dense gloom wherein they melted away. And in the very wonder of this, it would be itself again, distinct and clear as ever."

- **A Christmas Carol**, Charles Dickens

COLIN QUASHIE

CHAPTER 1

4 years earlier

 Dr. Hamilton loathed flying. The queasiness in the pit of his stomach threatened to erupt with each step taken down the winding tunnel ramp toward the cabin door where flight attendants greeted passengers with counterfeit smiles and rehearsed welcomes before rerouting them by seating. Disquieted by the growing nausea, when asked for his seat assignment, he could do little more than stare stupidly ahead.

"I'm, I'm sorry," he stuttered.

Fumbling to produce the boarding pass, he dropped his carry-on and apologized yet again while kneeling to gather his scattered belongings.

"It's okay, sir, take your time," said Beverley Tynes, the only attendant coming to his aide. A comely young woman in her mid 30's, she had a flawless smile accompanying her patient demeanor.

"I had it just a second ago," he mumbled, "I know it's here

somewhere." Looking around, he suddenly became aware of the condescending glances from the other passengers, which reinforced the general notion that he was every bit the disheveled, senile, 75 year old scientist he appeared to be. The rising chorus of impatience caused by the bottleneck he had created echoed in the tunnel and quickly replaced whatever fear he was experiencing with embarrassment.

Sensing the growing irritation, and knowing they had a full compliment of passengers yet to seat, Beverley intervened by pulling the boarding pass from its hiding place behind his pocket protector.

"Dr. Charles Hamilton, seat 6a. That's a First Class berthing. It's the window seat straight ahead on your left. Here," she said standing, then aiding him to his feet, "let me help you with your belongings. Welcome aboard."

Beverley led him to his seat, stowed his carry-on and hung his overcoat in the forward closet before returning.

"My name is Beverley Tynes and I'll be your flight attendant. May I get you something to drink, Dr. Hamilton?"

This was his first time flying First Class, and therefore, was unfamiliar with the benefits afforded the upper echelon.

"Uh, Coke, with very little ice, please."

"I'll be back in a moment."

He set about trying to decipher the innovative controls of the spacious seat, but after a maddening minute, gave up. With his tortuous boarding experience still fresh in his mind, he was reluctant to seek any more assistance and resigned himself to the fact that were he to fall asleep, it would be in the upright position.

The answer to his dilemma soon arrived in the form of

another passenger who took the aisle seat, 6B. The gentleman introduced himself, quickly nestled in, and then navigated the controls with such ease and dexterity it amazed the doctor. Appreciative of the unsolicited assistance, he mimicked 6B's actions, reclined and breathed a sigh of relief just as Beverley returned with his drink.

"Here you are, sir. Coke, very little ice."

"Thank you."

Dr. Hamilton stared out the window as the airplane backed away from its berth and began its slow trek toward the runway. He listened with little interest at the flight attendant's safety instructions, acted out in concert with the overhead video, and instead focused his attention on the letter he held in his hands. Received a month earlier, he had read it every day since, and by now had committed its text to memory. Nonetheless, he unfolded and read it again.

> Dr. Hamilton; It is the Nobel Prize Committee's distinct privilege to inform you that you have been selected as this year's recipient of the Nobel Prize in Medicine. Your pioneering research in the area of neurochemistry and the subsequent influential effect of specific organic compounds on the micro-management of synaptic transmitters has resulted in greater understanding of neural processes and given valuable insight into the analysis and prognosis of behavioral anomalies. Your achievements have benefited mankind and set new standards in the field of medicine. We invite you

to join us on this historic occasion to
be lauded by your peers.

It was a dream realized. The culmination of a labor of love he had endured for nearly 50 years. He never imagined his research would receive much interest, but now that it had, he was both humbled and pleased.

He refolded the letter, took a sip of his drink and closed his eyes with satisfaction as the plane taxied into position for take off. Moments later, the thrust of the engine's huge jets opened full throttle, sending the plane speeding down the runway and easing it effortlessly into the evening sky.

As a scientist, he understood the physics behind flight, but remained awed by its wonder. Looking out the port window, he watched the carpet of city lights tilt from side to side and grow smaller as the plane executed a series of banking maneuvers before settling onto a course taking them towards the coastline. As they gained altitude, the blanket of lights ended sharply, intersected jaggedly by the dark plateau he knew to be the ocean, but could no longer verify by waves dotting the surface. Only a few small boats and what he assumed was a cruise ship blemished the inky monotony with sporadic dots of light.

Pointed due east across the Atlantic, the plane finally settled onto it's cruising altitude. The fading western light granted access to the brightest stars and silhouetted the massive wing of the jumbo jet knifing through the cold, thin air.

"We'll be handing out dinner menus shortly. Would you like another drink," asked Beverley.

"If you don't mind, the same thing, Coke --"

"With very little ice," she finished, taking his empty glass. Grateful for her earlier assistance, he followed her with his eyes and silently hoped that someone as pleasant and beautiful as she had someone special in her life.

His gaze soon returned to the window. In the dark distance, he could barely make out the edges of a large cloudbank erratically illuminated by lightning. He squinted and watched closely for the one burst long and bright enough to reveal the formations true dimensions.

As a child, he and his sister would lie in open fields and make a game of staring at the rapidly forming cumulonimbus clouds prevalent during the height of the summer season. They awarded each other one point for every shape matched with known objects or people. He especially enjoyed watching the clouds slowly morph into other shapes, and then trying to guess what they would briefly become before continuing to shape shift. You got two points for that. How wondered many points she would have awarded him for seeing a shape in an intermittently lit cloud at night?

As the lightning intensified, he believed he could make out the face of a woman and anxiously bobbed between two windows for a better view of the next burst to prove him correct. The cloudbank appeared to be moving closer and he anticipated the Captain altering course. Flying through it was not an option. Formations of that magnitude were nature's way of cooling the earth and generated high winds caused by the updrafts from the warm ocean below. It was certainly no place for an airplane to be.

His fear was quickly realized with the first rumble of turbulence, followed by the return of nausea in the pit of his stomach. A few seconds later, the plane lurched again. The display lights flashed as the warning 'pong' sounded throughout the cabin, preceding the Captain's voice on the loud speakers.

"This is your Captain speaking. It appears we've hit a little patch of turbulence. For those of you up and about, please return to your assigned seats and fasten your seat belts. We should be out of this before you know it and you can get back to counting those flying sheep. Sorry if I woke you up; thank you." His attempted levity at the end of the broadcast was meant to dispel fear, but did little to reassure many.

Following the Captain's order, Dr. Hamilton pulled at the loose end of his seat belt until it was snug against his lap. He did so just in time. The airplane lifted violently, then dropped and pitched in a series of convulsive maneuvers. Any drinks, reading material or electronic gear left unattended went careening into laps and into the aisles.

As the turbulence intensified, he peered out to see if they had foolishly ventured into the approaching storm and fixated on the portion of the cloudbank, now closer than ever, that looked like the woman's face. A large burst of lightning danced behind its features and sure enough, there she was, a surly, chubby faced woman staring directly at him before vanishing.

Unable to get to her seat during the commotion, Beverley was forced to seek refuge by clutching the edge of the pantry sink with one hand and the curtain rod with the other, while using both feet to pin herself securely against a cabinet door. As the plane continued to shudder and roll, she didn't dare move and held on for dear life until moments later, the plane steadied out and calm restored.

She sighed relief and relaxed her grip. After straightening her uniform and examining her appearance, she checked to see what, if anything, the turbulence had displaced. Nothing major. Good. A quick nod and a gesture of 'OK' from Penney, the other First Class flight attendant, reassured her that everything was taken care of in their section. She poured Dr. Hamilton's drink, collected a stack of dinner menus, and then headed into the cabin to serve the passengers. Finding Dr. Hamilton's seat vacated, she pulled out his tray table and placed the drink on it, along with a dinner menu.

"Excuse me, I didn't order a drink," said passenger '6B', assuming she'd placed it there because his tray table was hosting a laptop.

"That's for Dr. Hamilton."

"Who?"

"Dr. Hamilton; the gentleman in the window seat," she clarified.

'6B' glanced at the empty seat then quizzically at Beverley.

"But there's no one sitting there."

"He's probably in the bathroom."

"I'm sorry, but that seat has been empty since we lifted off. There's no one sitting there," he reiterated with a hint of annoyance.

It was rude, to say the least, to argue with a passenger. As training and experience had taught, she signaled agreement with a courteous smile, and then continued handing out the menus. On the way back to the galley, she glanced at the bathroom and saw that it was unoccupied, but nonetheless, pushed open the door to verify its vacancy.

Anxious to prove passenger '6B' wrong, she ventured into Business Class to see if the doctor was perhaps using their bathroom or standing somewhere in the aisle. He was nowhere to be seen and upon approach, she noticed another passenger exiting the bathroom.

Curiosity was getting the better of her and suggested she embark on a pilgrimage throughout Coach class in search of her missing passenger. There was no sight of him there either.

After returning to First Class, she feigned stowage of a blanket to check the overhead bin where she had personally placed his carry on and saw that it was empty. She walked forward and checked the closet for his overcoat . . . it too was missing. With the mystery deepening, Beverley decided to consult the definitive source for answers.

The passenger manifest hung on a clipboard just inside the galley curtain. She quickly scanned the seating assignments and was surprised to see that passenger '6B' was correct. According to the log, seat 6a was empty. She leafed through the alphabetized list of passenger names, then the amended page of stand-by's, and found no one by the name of Hamilton listed. She rechecked the list using his first name, Charles, just in case there was some error. That too proved unsuccessful.

According to the manifest, there were 330 passengers on board. She walked the length of the plane slowly down the port aisle, taking a mental count of the passengers while scanning each face, then made her way forward up the starboard aisle until returning to First Class. The count was correct. *330 passengers.*

Confused and slightly disoriented, she closed her eyes, sighed and tried to come to grips with an incredibly disturbing thought. Dr. Charles Hamilton, seated in seat 6a on Sky Trans flight 8510 to London, had been nothing more than a figment of her imagination.

CHAPTER 2

Three weeks before Christmas

 He had a well-earned reputation as a humorless man. Even so, the notion there existed people who thought Chippendale was an exotic dancer made him roll with laughter until it brought tears to eyes more proficient at spotting prey.

After all, Ernest Anthony Bell III was an aristocratic snob. A 'blue blood' of the deepest indigo, he was born and carefully bred on one of the South's oldest, and questionably, largest plantations. Long before his entry into the waiting world, plans had been made to safeguard the family trust against any potentially wasted life after the cradle. This foresight insured that whatever oak shrouded lane he chose to wander on his way to the grave would be evenly paved with gold.

His upbringing was severe. The rigid discipline of military boarding schools reinforced by proxy his father's desire that he be well educated and indoctrinated with the tacit understanding that life by nature was cruel. The elder statesman believed that in order to thrive, not just survive, one had to adopt and practice a ruthless economic ethos that over time would ultimately become the deciding factor in separating the truly wealthy from the simply rich. God may have deeded the earth to the meek, but if he owned the most habitable parts of it, they would eventually have to lease from him.

After his fathers passing, Ernest fully embraced the capitalistic gospel and preached its sermon worldwide. He had expanded the family business beyond his father's dreams, and in so doing, had amassed a fortune so vast and diversified he once considered petitioning for statehood.

From high atop his opulent penthouse suite, the singular thing that had consumed his very existence, money, kept him occupied. Tonight however, instead of being on the receiving end, he was giving it away. Every single bit of it down to the last dollar, euro, pound and peso.

Cases of rare coins and jewels sat alongside stacks of ledgers, yearly reports, deeds and other various and sundry financial paperwork, towering in mountainous piles on the massive oak desk. So bunkered was Ernest that he was nearly obscured from view as he furiously punched the keys of an adding machine like an auditor charged with finding stolen funds. The unbroken stream of tape inching from the desktop calculator fell like a waterfall collecting in a foot high pool of curled summation on the floor, its length confirming his wealth.

Finally, the whir of the calculator stopped. He examined the total, stood, and then ripped the tape from the machine with a flourish.

"Two billion, eight hundred twenty-three million, seven

hundred forty-two thousand, five hundred and twenty-two dollars and fifty-nine cents!" he declared. "And that's just the liquid assets!"

Suddenly, like a deranged thief, he ransacked the piles of holdings on his desk, tossing them aside haphazardly, until he found his checkbook. Using his arm as a broom, he swept the remaining items from the desk in one swift motion and then began to make out a check for the aforementioned total.

"When the stock, bonds, t-bills and trusts are liquidated, I should clear somewhere between 25 and 30 billion!" he proclaimed loudly as Handel's 'Messiah' filled the lavish suite with the only reminder of Christmas.

Standing abruptly, he ripped the check from the ledger, slammed it down on the table and bellowed, "Easy come, easier gone!" Satisfied with his only act of charity, he began to soft shoe around the penthouse.

"I can't believe how wonderful it feels to be poor. My father was right. 'Poverty of purpose is worse than poverty of purse!' All these years I've been miserable, consumed with the thought of making more money than I could possibly spend in a hundred lifetimes. Now, I feel like a child again!"

Perhaps it was the euphoria of a new challenge or the physical exertion brought on by the nostalgic giddiness of a child immune to an illness others recognized as life's hardships, one could not tell. Nevertheless, something was making him sweat profusely and grow lightheaded.

"Perhaps it's just me, but is it hot in here?" he asked.

The question, panted through thin, clean-shaven lips between mops of his brow with a silk kerchief, remained unanswered by the marble busts and proud portraits of southern heroes.

"I must be coming down with something. Either that, or the heat," he surmised with a glance at the roaring fireplace. "I'll just open the doors and cool this place down a bit."

He steadied himself on the corner of the desk to catch his breath and clear his head, and then stumbled towards the French doors leading to the veranda. With shaking, liver spotted hands, he pulled back the tapestry serving as curtains and reached for the gold plated handles. Once opened, he took a deep breath of the cool, crisp night air scented with the seasonal odor of confederate jasmine, salt and the stench of the surrounding marshland.

The cool breeze embraced him and quickly accomplished its mission on both fronts. It cooled the suite while clearing the lightness from his head and reinvigorated his senses.

"I can't wait until the morning! If a picture is worth a thousand words, the look on my accountant's face will be a priceless first edition when he hears that I'm giving away all my money!"

Anxious to capitalize on the feeling, he stepped fully onto the veranda, taking stock of the clear night sky and the view of the harbor where a container ship was slowly snaking its way up the snaking river. If one pill works wonders, why not take another.

He took in a deeper breath and held it before exhaling loudly. He suddenly grew lightheaded again, then stumbled and grabbed the iron railings for support. His breathing was becoming shallower as his body beaded with sweat.

"It must be twenty odd degrees out here," he wheezed between rattling heaves, "Yet I'm sweating like a Derby winner.

I can't seem to cool down."

In an attempt to regain his equilibrium, he shook his head furiously and stretched his scrawny arms to take in more air. In his growing delirium, the lights of the historic skyline began to blur, further complicated by the stinging sweat now rolling into and clouding his eyes. He wiped his face with his sleeve, and then began disrobing to cool off further.

Though under duress, his sensitive breeding had not completely abandoned him. He neatly folded each piece of clothing before placing them on the wrought iron table.

Naked, with the exception of silk boxers, he clutched the railing and looked down at the blue street level awning, which in his hallucinatory state appeared as, "A pool! I bet that feels cool on a hot, humid night like tonight."

The sight of the water returned him to his imagined youth. He nimbly climbed upon the railing, laughing like a happy child unburdened by the cares of the world, then looked back and called out to imaginary friends who were obviously waiting for their garrulous leader to test the waters temperature and depth.

"C'mon, let's jump in!" The marble busts and static subjects in the paintings looked on with pompous indifference, as if daring him to jump.

"All of y'all are chickens! Last one in is a rotten egg!"

He pinched his nose, stepped off the railing and pulled his knees into his chest like a fat child doing a cannonball dive. He was plummeting to his sure death, all the while giddy with fatal remembrance.

The canvas awning, sturdy enough to survive the pummeling winds of Hurricane Hugo and its less intense siblings, was never designed to handle this new threat to it's strength and durability. Without apology or fanfare, it immediately collapsed under the weight of the laughing meteor. In a final show of respect to his standing in the community, the edges of the canopy folded inward and completely covered him like a warm blanket against the cold.

The only audience to the late night drama had a somewhat accessory point of view. A pair of red leather pumps, stuffed with large feet wearing matching red stockings, stood on the edge of the veranda. Next to them, a red, wool, floor length cape better suited for the elements draped alongside.

By the time startled screams reached their ears, both figures had retreated into the warmth of the abandoned suite. A fleshy hand accessorized with laced gloves silently scooped up the first, last and only act of charity by Ernest Anthony Bell III and deposited it into a purse for safekeeping.

Moments later, a stiff breeze filled the penthouse, scattering the remaining papers and leaving the marble busts and portraits to contemplate whom their new owners would be.

CHAPTER 3

Two weeks before Christmas

 One look at Austen Fisher's bedroom and it was plain to see that she was not a typical six-year-old girl. For one, it was disturbingly neat. Her bed, though covered with an inordinate amount of decorative pillows, would easily have passed inspection by a Marine Drill Sergeant. At the foot of it lay a neatly folded quilt with her name appliquéd in colorful fabrics, a different one for each letter.

The surroundings were void of the many trappings and decor typical of a child her age. There was no chest filled with broken or unused toys, nor were there any traces of the latest video games. Corporate marketing of the latest child stars and comic book movie characters remained unaccounted for. Instead, her creative endeavors adorned the soft pastel colored walls of the room. Crayon portraits of smiling faces gleaned from an active imagination and fueled by a budding desire to one day become an artist were spaced and hung evenly. Pictures of foreign places and people she found interesting filled remaining spaces. Complimenting them was a small television sitting on top of a DVD player next to a rack of educational discs and children's versions of classic tales.

Considering the fact that she alone was responsible for her room's daily housekeeping and did so without any prodding from her father, spoke to a personality that any child psychologist would easily diagnose as obsessive compulsive disorder caused by the latent onset of trauma. Perhaps, but in her words, it simply made whatever she was looking for easier to find.

The monarch of the realm sat patiently scrutinizing the contents of her latest letter to Santa Claus. After making whatever grammatical and typographical checks a six-year-old was capable of making, she began reading aloud the contents.

"Dear Mr. Santa Claus, My name is Austen Fisher. I am six years old now. I still live in Charleston, South Carolina at fifty-one Carolina Place. It is the duplex with the oak tree in the yard. I am writing you again because you keep forgetting to bring me what I want for Christmas. My daddy say you don't answer letters because you are not really real like the Easter bunny and the toot fairy. He said only polar bears and snowmen live in the North Pole because it is cold. He said people would freeze like Popsicles if they lived there. My mommy said you were real, but since you never answer my letters, maybe daddy is right. You are just make beleive. This is the last time I will write you. If you are really real, please bring me what I want for Christmas. It is the same as last year and the year before that, Austen Fisher"

Satisfied with her prose, she folded the letter neatly, placed it in an envelope, sealed, and then addressed it:

Mr. Santa Claus, The North Pole, USA

She stuck two stamps on it, and then turned it over in her hands and inspected it again. After a few moments, she realized something was missing: her return address.

A Fisher, 51 Carolina Place,
Charleston, SC 29403

She wanted no excuses. This was the last time she would write. If he existed, she wanted Santa Claus to get her letter so he would know exactly how she felt and where he needed to be on December the 25th at midnight sharp. With two weeks to go, it should get there in plenty of time for him to read.

Though she did not state exactly what she wanted for Christmas, she had done so last year and the year before that. It had not changed. Since he could remember the name of every boy and girl as well as if they had been naughty or nice, he would know who she was, and what she wanted. If he were really Santa Claus, he or one of his elves . . . his elves, hmmm. Maybe that's what happened. One of his elves had read the letter and forgot to tell Santa. For clarity's sake, she added in red crayon to both sides:

For Mr. Santa Claus himself only!

She then underlined it with black for added emphasis.

Pleased with her efforts, she ran downstairs and carefully placed the letter in the mailbox, address side up, and then raised the flag and checked to see if the mailman was at hand before making her way inside. From the safety of her room, she sat in her rocking chair and watched from her window overlooking the street.

She was about to doze off to sleep when the familiar bark of Ms. Margaret's Schnauzer, Hank, announced the arrival of Tim, the mailman. He was Hank's favorite because he cared enough to carry a pocket full of dog treats, which he generously dispensed. Spoiled by the daily routine, Hank kept a steady vigil and wailed with impatience at the first sight of the carrier.

Hank was not the only one interested. Austin ran out to the mailbox and watched as Tim followed a familiar path that took him down the other side of the street before turning and heading her way. She removed the letter and inspected it again as he arrived and handed her a folded stack of circulars and letters.

"Hello, Austen, how are you today?" he greeted.

"I'm fine, Mr. Tim. Here," she said handing him her precious cargo.

He looked at the address and smiled. "Wow, pretty important stuff. I'll have to make sure this goes out this afternoon so it can get to Santa in time for Christmas."

"Thank you," said Austen smiling.

"You're welcome."

She remained at the gate following him with her eyes as he finished delivering the mail to the rest of the houses on the street. It wasn't that she didn't believe him; she just wanted to see her mission through and waved as he drove by. She kept watch until his van disappeared around the corner before heading inside to give her father the mail.

Inside the mail facility, Tim scooped the handful of letters to Santa from his mailbag and began the tortuous task of shredding them. How many letters to Santa had he shredded in the seventeen years he had worked at the Post Office? *There were far too many to count.* In that time, he had never been able to reconcile the contradiction between his sworn oath to deliver the mail with his inclination to destroy their letters and violate the trust placed in him by children so young. He spent a moment staring at each letter as though seeking absolution before inserting them into the whirring steel blades. Considering the amount of hope, prayers, dreams, fantasy and desperation written on the pages within, he owed them that much.

He knew all the children on his route by name and marveled how closely their penmanship matched their personalities. Lula Porter's light script and crisp thin lines illustrated her shyness, while Towne Barber's large, bold font preference mirrored the confidence of a gregarious prankster. In certain terms, Austen's underlined text demanded delivery. It underscored her seriousness at such a young age and reminded him how fleeting youth's innocence could be.

This would be her last letter. Somewhere between now and next year, she would realize who and what Santa Clause was. As baby teeth surrender to permanent ones, her literal belief in Santa would succumb to a figurative interpretation of the 'Spirit of Giving' and like everyone else she'd accept Santa

Claus for what he really was; a necessary lie parents tell children out of love and a need to have them learn the moral tale of the importance of giving.

Standing there staring at Austen's letter dredged up memories. He used to help his daughter Zoe write her letters to Santa and followed each with a promise to make sure Santa received it, not because he was her father, but because he had taken an oath to deliver the mail 'through rain or shine.' He used to assure her that the oath also covered the 'sleet and snow' of the North Pole, so there was no need to worry. Santa would get her letter, and she would get her presents.

He hoped that Austen's father, Arthur, knew the contents of the letter and out of the love he possessed for her, would assume the responsibility of delivery the Post Office was forced to abdicate. Sadly, he dropped her letter into the teeth of the insatiable metal beast and watched as it was cross cut into a million pieces, then unceremoniously collected in the clear plastic bag labeled 'recycle'.

His shift over, Tim made the slightest of detours on his way to the parking lot and tossed the bag of shredded letters into the dumpster labeled 'recycle.'

The post office recycle dumpster was emptied once a week, but during the busy holiday season, service was increased to twice a week. The truck usually came in the afternoon, so it was highly unusual for one to arrive shortly after midnight.

The guard staffing the security booth first noticed it on his array of camera monitors, and then personally spotted it when it turned into the driveway. He zipped his jacket, angled a nightstick into its holster, grabbed a walkie-talkie and flashlight, and then exited the booth in anticipation of the unexpected arrival.

Standing behind the gate arm, he checked the log and saw that no pick-ups or deliveries were scheduled. The only addendum was a post-it note reminding him to buy a lottery ticket when he got off work. The jackpot had reached 230 million dollars and the thought of winning that kind of money two weeks before Christmas made him sigh.

Looking up from the log, he let out a hiccup and jerked with surprise at the sight of the truck's grill poised inches away from his face on the other side of the gate arm. *Strange, I didn't hear it pull up.* The truck's dimmed headlights left only the amber fog lights and green running lights to identify the nondescript vehicle. The light over the entrance gate offered little assistance to the guard and instead reflected glare off the darkened windshield obscuring the driver or any movement within the truck's cab.

The guard adjusted his hat and holster involuntarily in a bid to regain his composure. He stepped around the gate toward the driver side, switched on his flashlight and raised the beam high enough to illuminate the driver's face without shining the beam directly into his eyes. In a move clearly defying his authority, the tinted side window remained sealed.

As he angled the flashlight's beam higher, a slight twinge of fear began to stir in his loins. He stiffened and nervously raised his hand to the hilt of his nightstick. Suddenly, a wave of relief swept over him. He relaxed and felt rather foolish in the same way you do when you finally match a forgotten name with the familiar face of an old friend.

Smiling and waving recognition, he raised the gate, lowered the tire spikes and stood aside as the truck glided by. He gave no thought whatsoever to how a truck so large could pass without making a sound as if floating on the wind. He watched as it silently stopped in front of the recycle dumpster, emptied the contents into its cavity, then turned and exited as silently as it had arrived.

He waved goodbye to his old friend, raised the spikes, lowered the gate's arm and returned to the security booth with only a single memory of the event remaining in his head . . . exactly how would he spend 230 million dollars if he did win the lottery?

The same sequence of events played out across the city until the first hint of day glowed in the east. The truck arrived at the airport, cleared its tenacious levels of security with the same ease as the post office and proceeded to the far end of the fenced property. Waiting patiently on the tarmac for the truck's arrival was a cargo plane equally as nondescript. Upon arrival, the airplane's transport ramp lowered, allowing access to its spacious interior. The truck backed in, deposited its stuffed container and drove forward exiting the airplane. A series of automated rollers on the floor of the aircraft raised and positioned the latest load neatly alongside others similarly stowed containers, then quietly raised its ramp and prepared for take-off.

Air traffic controllers were unwittingly eager to grant runway access. Equally as naïve, pilots of departing flights awaiting take-off smiled and waved recognition as the airplane taxied past and took its place at the head of the flight line.

Moments later, it quietly eased into the morning light without registering so much as the faintest of blips on any radar system known to man.

Far above the Arctic Circle, the plane appeared clearly on the North Pole's radar system. Cleared for landing by tower attendants, the airplane touched down without incident on the smooth sheet of runway ice and glided to a halt next to a team of elves wearing red jump suits.

The airplane's cargo was unloaded onto waiting transport trucks. A van with flashing red lights escorted the precious freight into a cavernous building where another team of efficient elves quickly went about their business of off-loading the containers. The bags were stacked on palettes and fork lifted deeper into the facility where they were sliced open and emptied into a large hopper and siphoned downward onto a fluttering conveyor belt. Every flake of paper slowly made its way toward a series of mechanical arms that raked and sifted the fragments into a single layer.

Passing under the watchful eyes of elves fussing over the chards of paper like worker bees, any hint of refuse was picked from the conveyor with gloved hands before entering a sealed unit, which reconfigured the letters (in a secret process which will not be revealed here), and restored them whole to pristine accuracy.

Each envelope was scanned, bar coded, time stamped and then routed through mechanical gates by zip code. Sharp rotating knives opened the envelopes, removed and unfolded the contents, digitally scanned and recorded the names, addresses and presents requested, and then carefully bundled and sealed them by lot for filing.

Austen's letter was halfway through the process when an alarm sounded. It was plucked off the line, placed in a clear round container and deposited into a vacuum tube that sucked it skyward through a succession of clear pipes. Its journey ended at the desk of an elderly, wizened faced elf wearing reading glasses.

As he read Austen's letter, a concerned look crossed his face. He sat back in his chair, took off his glasses, rubbed his eyes and shook his head. After toying with the curls in his white beard, he lurched forward, stamped the letter and envelope 'URGENT REVIEW', then placed both inside a lined manila interoffice envelope and wrote, 'Verna - Corporate, 112th Floor – URGENT REVIEW', on the next available line. He stood, waddled out of his office and placed the envelope in the clear clamshell on the outside of his cubicle.

Moments later, Chip, a young messenger elf, picked up the envelope and seeing it marked 'URGENT REVIEW', took off running through the maze of cubicles at breakneck speed.

Chip narrowly escaped harm as he deftly navigated through the tangle of traffic on his motorized snowboard until he reached his destination. He skidded to a halt, hopped off and darted inside the lobby of the Peppermint Plaza, a soaring glass building emblazoned with the placard, 'Christmas Industries - Corporate Headquarters'. He sprinted erratically through the bustle of employees toward the bank of elevators and squeezed his way inside the first available car just as the doors were closing to the annoyance of packed passengers inside.

He disembarked on the 112th Floor. Acutely aware of his surroundings, he brushed off his feet, removed his hat and respectfully slowed his pace as he made his way through the maze of hallways trying not to draw too much attention to himself from the professionally suited elder elves milling about the corporate corridors. Finally arriving at the packages' destination, he checked his appearance once more, and then slowly entered the spacious outer office of Santa Claus.

"Merry Christmas, how may I help you?" quizzed Verna, Santa's Executive Secretary, without looking up.

"Merry Christmas, ma'am. I have a delivery from Receiving."

She glanced up, beckoned him forward with a wave of her hand and received the package with a concerned smile.

"Thank you. Merry Christmas."

"Merry Christmas to you too, ma'am."

She waited for him to leave, then opened the manila envelope and read Austen's letter. *Not another one, Santa is not going to like this.*

After returning the letter to the envelope, she entered Santa's office and gently placed the letter in his 'in-box'.

THE PRESENT

"Come in!" exclaimed the Ghost. "Come in and know me better, man! I am the Ghost of Christmas Present. Look upon me! You have never seen the like of me before!"

- A Christmas Carol, Charles Dickens

COLIN QUASHIE

CHAPTER 4

 The tilt of the earth may have submerged the North Pole in complete darkness during much of the winter months, but it was far from that. The icy metropolis was awash in a sea of lights from above and below.

The aurora borealis (Northern lights) was particularly bright. The sky swayed with curtains of neon green, yellow and red that both complimented and competed with the luminous blanket of city lights spread out far beneath.

Mountainous glacial peaks cradled the city. On their lower slopes, forests of Christmas Pines covered with mistletoe infused the crisp night air with the scent of cinnamon from their fragrant cones. Farther downward, the Pines gave way to fields of holly bushes and wild peppermint shrubs sprouting miniature candy canes.

Clusters of elfin lodges ringed the outskirts of the city, each subdivision distinctive, borrowing their layout from the unique shapes of snowflakes and named after seasonal iconography like Garland Farms, Tinsel Brook and Gingerbread Point.

Ice-covered lanes lit by oil lamps connected the cozy

hamlets. When viewed from above, their delicate design wove a symmetrical tapestry of form and function circling the bustling city center.

As far as the eye could see, Christmas literally hung in the air. Displays of every description celebrating Yule were suspended with the care human poets and writers had never witnessed, but imagined and wrote of anyway.

Laughter and song filled the air. Colorful wreaths and banners draped from every door and pole, snowmen graced every yard, twinkling lights dangled from every eave and ice sculptures glittered in every square.

Not ones to be outdone by their surroundings, the elfin inhabitants strolled the streets dressed in festive attire. They took in the sights of shops and storefronts displaying various seasonal wares produced by artisans as well as performances by roving troupes of entertainers.

The entire city pulsed with anticipation and buzzed with excitement as if the world was a gift, wrapped and waiting for children to tear it open and savor the good tidings they freely offered.

The person garnering the most attention may have been Santa Claus, but his most beloved employee - the Ghost of Christmas Present - enjoyed celebrity status as well.

The debonair Spirit cut a fashionable path as he strode confidently down the sidewalk. He wore a tailored red suit, starched white shirt and a red and white striped tie that complimented two toned patent leather shoes. Commanding the attention of all, he returned each greeting received with equal generosity.

Vincent, the doorman at Christmas Industries, anticipating the Spirit's arrival, cleared a path and held the door open.

"Good morning, Christmas Present. Merry Christmas, sir!" he said with a tip of his hat.

"Thank you. Merry Christmas to you too!"

"They're waiting for you straight ahead, sir," he said pointing the way.

The corporate lobby teemed with activity. Everyone scurried to complete any final arrangements necessary for the big night ahead, yet took time to greet Christmas Present and offer continued directional guidance.

"Good morning, Christmas Present, keep straight ahead, sir."

"Hello, Present, elevators directly ahead on the left."

"You're looking good as always, sir. Almost there."

As he strode past the bank of elevators, an attendant corralled and guided him into a waiting car, "Merry Christmas, sir." Before he could question the elf's motives, he was asked, "112 floor, sir?"

"Uh, yeah, 112th Floor."

"112th floor it is, sir. Thank you."

"You're welcome," answered Christmas Present, though he was not sure why. Before he had a chance to ask why they were headed to the 112th floor, they had arrived. The moment the doors opened, Claire, his secretary, immediately intercepted him.

"Good morning, sir. My, don't we look festive today."

"Good morning -- "

"Claire, your secretary, sir."

"Of course. Good morning, Claire."

Ignoring his bewildered look, she locked her arm in his and guided him through the spacious hallway.

"As you know sir, today is Christmas Eve."

"Who could forget that?" he snickered.

"Oh, you'd be surprised, sir," she said holding open an office door. Had he been paying closer attention instead of quizzically surveying his surroundings while responding to the many greetings tossed his way, he would have noticed the hand painted gold leaf moniker on the glass door identifying the office's occupant as, 'The Ghost of Christmas Present - Director of Human Relations.'

"Nice office!" he remarked upon entry.

"*Your* office is very nice, sir."

"My office?"

"Yes, sir. Your office."

The morning ritual ended, or from her perspective, started, the moment she seated him behind his desk. She knew exactly what was coming next and continued her activities while he spent the next minute quietly familiarizing himself with his surroundings.

He would rock back and forth in his chair, testing the spring and marvel silently at the fresh scent and feel of leather before sitting forward and running his hands back and forth across the desks lacquered top.

After that, he would open each drawer, view the minimal contents, then turn his attention toward the phone and slide it closer. The framed picture of he and Santa Claus would command his attention next. He would pick it up, stare at the smiling faces, recognize himself, and then like a light illuminating the darkness, it would all become apparent.

The surge of remembrance would produce a sigh of relief easily heard from Claire's outer office, regardless of whether the door was open or shut. This signal meant it was almost time to brief him on the day's events.

Next, he would walk about the office and look at the other pictures, mementos and awards he had received over the decades. He would read a framed copy of a letter from Raven Slade, the first child to ever write and thank Santa Claus for her gifts.

Eventually, the expansive view from his corner office window would command his attention. Upon entry, Claire would find him standing there, his back to her, looking out at the glowing landscape stretched beneath him like a flickering carpet and comment on the stunning view.

As Claire waited, a smile crept onto her face. Watching him at the window reminded her why he was so beloved. He was a child. Christmas and all the magic and wonder it embodied lived in him and burst forth like a fountain of youth each minute of every day, regardless of the season. His joy was lethally contagious and infected everyone he met.

To human children, Rudolph the Red Nosed Reindeer was the North Pole's unofficial mascot, but to elves young and old, the Ghost of Christmas Present embodied the spirit of Christmas. His exploits and misadventures became the fodder for supermarket tabloids and late night comedians. Marketing executives loved his appeal and splashed his face on billboards and television. His bobble head doll was an annual best seller and recently was on pace to outsell Santa Claus'.

At the start of her employment, he used to frustrate her to

no end. As his name, the Ghost of Christmas Present, suggested, he lived in the present, and therefore, had no real memory.

On a good day, he could retain a thought for four or five minutes, but that was a stretch. Anything beyond that was hopeless. All speech, thought and emotions would transfer to and become the sole possession of the Ghost of Christmas Past.

The process astounded Claire and proved a mystery more enduring than how Santa Claus managed to deliver gifts to every home in every time zone exactly at the stroke of midnight. Christmas Present remained as much a mystery to her today as he had been when they first met decades ago. He had no known family and could not tell of his origin. There was a possibility that Santa Claus knew, but if he did, he refused to say.

If anyone had answers, it was the Ghost of Christmas Past. But the thought of even approaching, much less asking that disagreeable Spirit anything, was not something Claire was even remotely looking forward to doing anytime soon.

The one thing she had learned over the decades was that stress would diminish Christmas Present's abilities. In a bid for self-preservation, she had learned to take everything in stride and make sure he felt as though everything was running smoothly, even if it was not.

"What a great view!" he exclaimed as he plopped down in his chair.

"I wouldn't get too comfortable, sir. Santa wants you in his office immediately."

Christmas Present leaped from his chair in half the time it

took him to sit.

"Santa Claus wants to see me?" he worried. "What for?"

"Verna, that's his Executive Secretary, didn't say."

He slowly sat and began to fidget nervously. Without the ability to remember, he had no reference point from which to judge his relationship with others. Had he done something wrong? Was Santa mad at him for some reason? Maybe he was getting another award.

He searched Claire's face for an answer, but saw nothing to indicate either way. She had mastered the art of concealing her emotions and offered him a smiling palette from which he could gather no indication whatsoever. After all, if he saw her upset, his ability to do his job effectively would diminish.

What he could never forget, because he was constantly reminded, was that Santa Claus was a very powerful man and a revered icon. Summons to a private meeting with him was hardly ever a good thing. Knowing how he would react to news of the meeting, Claire had prepared for it ahead of time.

"I'm not sure what this is all about, sir, so I jotted down some notes for you," she said handing him a series of questions and answers written on a stack of index cards. He thumbed through them voicing each aloud.

"My name is the Ghost of Christmas Present. I am the Director of Human Relations. I have worked in that capacity for 160 years. Our mission is to bring joy and happiness to every boy and girl and spread the spirit of Christmas throughout the world."

He would have stood there going through the notes until he was comfortable with his responses, but Claire knew that could take most of the morning and Santa was waiting. Considering it was Christmas Eve, he had little time, and less patience.

"Sir, I think you should be going. You do not want to keep Santa waiting. It's Christmas Eve and he has a very tight schedule."

Christmas Present took a deep breath and tried to steady his nerves. Claire used this opportunity to straighten his tie and reassure him that everything would be okay.

"You'll be fine, sir. Try not to speak unless spoken to and here," she said placing a pen in his pocket, "don't be afraid to jot down anything he says that you feel is important. OK?"

She guided him towards the door and with a final brush of his jacket, watched him off to see Santa Claus like a mother watching her child off to school for the first time.

He was barely into his journey when he stopped dead in his tracks. As usual, Claire anticipated the hesitation and waited for him to turn. The look on his face told her he had no idea where Santa's office was located. She pointed at the floor. He looked down, then back at her. "Follow the red line on the floor, it leads to Santa's office," she whispered aloud.

He looked down and noticed that he was indeed straddling a red line. He beamed a smile, gave her a knowing salute, then turned and continued on his way while continuing to thumb through his notes.

CHAPTER 5

The cab pulled up outside 49 Carolina Place and deposited a weary Beverley on the sidewalk. She had switched her domestic flight schedule with another flight attendant's international route in order to give the bride-to-be more time at home to plan her wedding. The longer hours granted her the rare opportunity to travel abroad along with precious days off during the holidays, but the strain was starting to show.

Beverley loved Christmas. She had grown up in a large family and the holidays were an especially fond time for her. Thanksgiving was a mini-reunion of sorts and she made it a point to never miss the family gathering. Christmas on the other hand was usually spent away from home and conversely, alone.

Her job had taken its toll on her relationships. At 35, she had been a flight attendant for 14 years, long enough for the romanticism of air travel to wane. A more sobering reality had replaced the notion that she was going to meet and fall in love with some handsome international jet setter. Most of the men she met were already married and those that were not had girlfriends and were simply looking for a layover date.

Whenever she did meet someone she considered nice, he usually lived in another city. Her flying privileges made it financially feasible for her to visit often, but coordinating her revolving schedule with her interest's time off meant the long the distance relationship had little chance of blooming into anything serious since they could never spend enough time together to take it to the next level. Eventually, the passion would cool. Phone calls that once came twice a day eased to every other day, then once a week, signaling the end was near.

She had fallen victim to the consummate cycle that had betrayed many young women. After college, she had concentrated on building a career. By her late 20's, she felt ready to commit to a serious relationship, but by then, the men she regarded as her peers were either married or divorced with kids and had no intention of getting serious anytime soon.

She often thought about using the Internet to find that special someone, but the dangers associated with that always haunted her. She met enough creeps trying to pick her up on a daily basis, keenly aware that many of them regarded her as a mile high waitress or bartender whose job consisted of handing out peanuts and drinks. Frustrated, she had simply decided to give up. *Oh well, when you quit looking, that's when it happens.*

The one thing she was looking forward to was time off. She still had the bulk of her Christmas shopping to do, but was not too concerned about that. She had already bought gifts for most of the people on her list in town and would wrap those later on that night, and then deliver them tomorrow. Everyone else was out of town and she would put those in the mail after Christmas.

After lugging her baggage up the brick path to her door, she made a return trip to the mailbox to check her mail and then remembered that Austen promised to pick it up and hold it for her. She was at the age where she craved responsibility and it gave Beverley an excuse to see her little friend. She had a surprise for her.

Austen must have sensed Beverley thinking about her because no sooner had Beverley returned to her porch than Austen appeared at the front door on her side of the duplex and peeked out.

"Hi, Ms. Beverley."

"Hello, Austen, how've you been? Come here and give me a hug."

Austen was more than willing to oblige. She ran out and wrapped her arms tightly around Beverley's waist.

"I missed you," said Beverley as she returned the hug and stroked Austen's hair.

"I missed you, too," said Austen releasing her grip. "Where'd you go this time?"

"A couple of places. Hmmm, let's see if you can figure this one out. It's an Asian country known as the 'land of the rising sun'. The capital city used to be called Edo, but now, it's called Tokyo . . ."

"Japan!" screamed Austen.

"That's right! And guess what?"

"What?"

"I brought something for you."

"Really?" asked Austen. Her eyes grew big at the promise of a surprise.

Beverley purposely took her time opening her luggage to retrieve the gift. She feigned clumsiness as Austen fidgeted.

"I know it's here somewhere. I hope I didn't forget and leave it on the plane."

The anticipation on Austen's face was palpable, causing Beverley to smile at the excitement she was generating. "Uh-oh, what's this, is that it?" she questioned with a surprised look. Like a magician pulling a rabbit from a hat, she snatched the gift from her carry-on and handed it to Austen, now beside herself with glee.

"Thank you, Miss Beverley. Thank You. I have something for you too."

"You do?"

"Yep!" said Austen and quickly darted inside. She returned moments later with Beverley's bundle of mail neatly arranged according to size.

"I checked the mailbox everyday just like you asked me to."

"Thank you. I really appreciate this," replied Beverley cradling the bundle.

She could tell by the way Austen looked at and ran her hand over the gift that she wanted to open it and warned, "That's your Christmas present, you can't open it until tomorrow. Okay? Put it under the tree with your other gifts."

Beverley winced as Austen's smile receded. She had committed a tragic error and regretted it instantly. Like a cosmic force voicing disapproval, the timer on Beverley's Christmas display activated, lighting her half of the duplex and further illuminating the mistake.

Beverley glanced up and took in a sight the neighborhood was accustomed to seeing during the holiday season; a single overhead porch light at 51 Carolina Place. In the three years she had lived next to the Fishers, no recognition of Christmas had ever surfaced. It was the only dwelling on the street that refused to participate in the holiday.

Austen's father, Arthur, was not a coarse or callous man by any stretch of the imagination. Despite the lack of outward displays he was a doting father and insofar as anyone could see was succeeding in raising a happy, socially adjusted child that was well disciplined and respectful.

He played with Austen often and did his best to make sure she took part in activities with her many friends in the neighborhood. Earlier that year, Beverley had helped him stage a surprise birthday party complete with a magician dressed like a clown and an inflatable water slide set up in the front yard.

He was equally meticulous when it came to her education. Enrolled in a private school, the scope of Austen's intellectual curiosity always amazed Beverley. She was definitely not that smart at her age.

However, when it came to Christmas, Arthur's efforts flagged.

Eager to reclaim Austen's smile, Beverley offered, "What if I keep your present under my Christmas tree? That way you can come over tomorrow and we can bake some Christmas cookies and open our presents together. How about that?"

"Okay!" replied Austen, her smile returning.

Relieved, Beverley caressed her cheek and spontaneously remarked, "You have the prettiest smile."

A blast of cold wind broke the moment and reminded

Beverley she still had a lot to do. "I'll see you tomorrow, okay?"

"Okay," replied Austen weakly.

As Beverley retrieved her key and placed it in the lock, she realized that neither wanted the moment to end. Noting that she had some last minute shopping to do, she made the snap decision to ask Austen to accompany her. Arthur would not mind, and both of them would enjoy the outing. Being able to walk with Austen through the mall, exposing her to the remaining sights and sounds of Christmas would at least make it feel like Christmas Eve in the Fisher household, even if it didn't look the part.

"Austen . . . would you like to go Christmas shopping with me?"

Before she could finish her sentence, Austen belted, "Can I?"

"Of course you *can*, but we'll have to ask your dad, *may* you go," corrected Beverley. "Okay?"

"Okay!"

Beverley stifled a laugh as Austen darted inside to get permission from Arthur. She had a long list of gifts to buy, but would never find one more precious than the smile she had just placed on Austen's face.

CHAPTER 6

Christmas Present stood outside Santa Claus's office, and like everyone else venturing into the saintly domain, checked his appearance, took a deep breath to settle his nerves and tried to imagine what the encounter would be like.

He glanced at his notes a final time, and then slipped them into his jacket pocket and entered. He strode confidently across the red carpet to announce his arrival to Verna.

"Hello, my name is --"

"Go on in he's waiting for you," she said without bothering to look up.

Her abruptness caused all composure to escape him. *This cannot be good.* He felt imaginary beads of sweat forming on his brow and wiped them with the back of his hand.

He edged closer to the door guarding Santa's inner sanctum and gingerly turned the ornate knob. He peeked inside and saw Santa staring out the window. Christmas Present may have thought he had a great view, but Santa's seamless panoramic expanse made you feel like you were flying.

"Gorgeous isn't it," Santa remarked more than questioned.

"A-hem, yes sir."

He entered fully, eased the door shut, then quietly moved closer while fighting the urge to review his notes until he stood at the edge of Santa's desk. As if on cue, Santa turned abruptly, leaned against the window and openly stared at Christmas Present.

This was not the image of Santa Claus embraced by the world. Gone was the fat, jolly, silver-bearded icon donning a red suit with black boots and matching belt. In his place stood a fit looking executive wearing a red tracksuit as if on his way to a morning work out. His close-cropped silver hair, matching a neatly trimmed beard and mustache, accented a chiseled face that complimented the steely gaze boring a hole in Christmas Present.

Though casually dressed, he maintained the countenance of royalty and projected the authority of corporate power. Christmas Present both withered and straightened under the scrutiny of his intense gaze that remained as veiled as his words. Christmas Present didn't know whether to laugh or cry so instead, he found a spot on the desk half way between Santa's gaze and the floor and studied it while he waited for Ole Saint Nick to speak.

"I'll assume Claire provided you with notes to save my reminding you where you are. She's good about that," he said at last

"Uh, yes sir,"

"As for why you're here . . . " Santa pushed himself away from his repose against the window and contemplatively crossed to the wall on his left which supported a long glass case filled with pictures, keepsakes, mementos and prized awards. It was a shrine to his leadership and reflected the decades of guidance and inspiration he had provided. He lovingly panned the display as Christmas Present edged closer and stood beside his mentor.

"Present . . . Christmas is changing," he began in a somber tone. "It used to be simple, girls and dolls, boys and bikes. These days, it's all about computers and video games . . . things we don't make."

He opened the case, picked out a yellowing black and white picture of a larger man in a Santa suit standing in front of a small wooden structure. He ran his figure across the glass wistfully.

"That was my first workshop," he reminisced.

"Is that you standing out front?"

"Yeah . . . a hundred pounds heavier. I had to lose weight. High blood pressure and diabetes run in my family." He continued to stare at the photo and spoke slowly as if he were invoking words that held the power of nostalgia. "Back then I made everything myself and only needed one reindeer and a wooden sleigh to make my deliveries."

He broke off his stare, returned the picture to its resting place, and continued his tour.

"Over the decades, we certainly have grown. We now deliver to 140 countries and oversee the manufacture and distribution of more toys than any other company in the world."

Reality rudely snatched him from his reminiscence. He faced Christmas Present and argued, "If Christmas Industries wasn't a non-profit we'd be bigger than Microsoft, Time Warner and General Electric, combined! Did you know that?"

Ignorant of such facts and anxious to place the focus anywhere than where it was directed, at him, Christmas Present pointed to a picture of a stoic figure sitting at a desk.

"Who's that?"

"That's Charles Dickens. You don't remember him do you?"

Present closed his eyes and tried his best to contribute something, *anything* to the conversation. Disappointed at his inability, he shook his head 'no.'

"Nice guy, good writer. He's part of the reason I asked you here today."

"How's that, sir?"

"The Christmas he knew, loved, and wrote about with a little inspiration from us, has been fading over the decades."

Santa began to pace. Christmas Present had never seen him lose him composure. That is, as far as he could remember.

"We've been so concerned with growth, we've lost sight of what used to make Christmas special . . . customer service! Our goal has never been to compete with other corporations for revenue. It's always been about the children," expounded Santa as his pace quickened in tempo with the ramped up speech. "I used to climb down each and every chimney, now I have 'drop zones' and 'delivery specialists' who blanket a subdivision from a single rooftop. I can't tell you the last time I caught a kid out of bed who should've been sleeping!"

Christmas Present flinched when he pounded the edge of his desk for emphasis. "We're losing the hearts and minds of both parents and children alike! This year alone, I've received more letters, like this," he reached across his desk, picked up

Austen's letter and shook it at Christmas Present, "than in any other decade!"

Christmas Present took the letter and quickly read it as Santa took a seat and tried to regain his poise. He waited until Christmas Present was finished and answered the question before he had a chance to ask it.

"She's a good kid. Her dad is a caring parent. They've been through a lot together."

"May I ask what she requested for Christmas, sir?"

"That doesn't matter. What matters is that you find a way to reverse this trend. "

"Me?" Christmas Present was surprised at how fast he responded.

"Yes, you."

The corporate mantle of responsibility demanded action. After all, he had a business to run and a Board of Directors to answer to. Though a non-profit, Christmas Industries was the largest employer in the North Pole, responsible for the welfare of thousands of workers and their families, not to mention the millions of children depending on them to fulfill their mission statement.

Regardless of the way it may have sounded to an outsider, his fondness for the forgetful spirit was evident. Were it not, they would not have been having this conversation. He would simply have had Verna draft a memo to Claire and let her relay it to Christmas Present, but that would not have underscored how serious he was. Besides, he did not want Christmas Present to panic and start to imagine scenarios that did not exist. What he needed was to make sure his Director of Human Relations understood clearly that he wanted careful attention paid to a matter threatening the very livelihood and future survival of the North Pole. It was a tough assignment that called for tough love.

"As Director of Human Relations, this falls under your purview," he said staring into his hands. "I don't think I need to remind you how important this is."

Santa's eyes rose to meet his.

"Either you find a way to get some results, or I may be forced to make a few changes in the coming year . . . if you know what I mean."

"Yes, sir. I understand. Anything else, sir?"

"Just one more thing." He pressed the intercom on his phone. "Verna, please send in the Urgent File."

"The entire file, sir?" her response crackled through the loudspeaker.

"The entire file."

Before Santa could lean back in his chair, the side door of his office opened and a team of elves filed in dragging two large mailbags each and dropped them at Christmas Present's feet. By the time they were finished, he could no longer see the floor around him.

He opened one of the bags and grabbed a handful of letters. By his count, "There must be at least 25,000 letters here, sir."

"33,242, to be exact," Santa corrected.

"How am I supposed to review this many letters, sir?"

Santa stood up and checked his watch. He was going to be late for his morning workout.

"I suggest the same way we answer them . . . one letter at a time."

CHAPTER 7

Over the decades, there have been many versions of the classic Charles Dickens tale, 'A Christmas Carol.' First published in 1843, it has been adapted to theater, opera, radio, television and film, with the earliest known version produced by Thomas Edison.

Along with *'Miracle on 42nd Street,' 'How the Grinch Stole Christmas'* and *'It's a Wonderful Life,'* it had become a staple of seasonal programming. The version that garnered the most critical acclaim was the British film adaptation of 1951 starring Alastair Sim as the unrepentant miser, Ebenezer Scrooge. This is the version Arthur Fisher was supposedly watching from the comfort of his recliner. Instead, it was watching him.

As Arthur slept, he found himself dreaming and starring in his own adaptation of the classic. He stood in as Ebenezer Scrooge while the recently deposed Ernest Anthony Bell III was cast in the role of Jacob Marley's ghost.

The spirit of the rich man wore only the silk boxers he had on when he leaped from his balcony to his tragic death.

"What do you want of me?" cried Arthur.

"Much," replied Ernest.

"Who are you?"

"In life I was Ernest Anthony Bell the Third . . . now dead . . . the last."

Arthur stretched out his trembling hand and tried to touch the spirit, but it passed straight through the gaunt, transparent body.

"You don't believe in me?"

"No, I don't."

"Why do you doubt your senses?"

"Because any little thing affects them. You may be a bad dream caused by heartburn or an undigested piece of steak. You could be an extra glass of wine for all I know."

Ernest raised and clanged his chains loudly, followed by a screeching wail that shook Arthur to his core and sent him to his knees trembling in fear.

"Spiritless man! Do you believe in me or not?"

"Mercy! I do, I do," cried Arthur. "But why do you trouble me?"

"It is required. I am condemned to wander the earth and witness in death what I refused to look upon in life. Doomed to behold what I cannot share, but might have shared and turned to happiness. Oh, woe is me!" Ernest lamented woefully.

"Why are you chained?"

"I wear the chain I forged in life. I made it link-by-link, and yard-by-yard. I gladly wore it of my own free will. Oh were you to know the length and heft of the one you forge," warned Ernest pitifully. "It was twice as long and heavy as mine just last Christmas. Yet still you labor on it. It is a *ponderous creation."*

"How can this be?"

"I cannot say as yet. Very little is permitted to me, for I cannot linger."

Ernest began gathering his length of chains and heaved them over his shoulder as he turned to leave.

"Hey, wait! What about me? What am I supposed I do?"

Slowly fading as he walked away, Ernest repeated, "Awake, Arthur, awake . . . wake up!

"Wake up. What's that supposed to mean?"

It meant Austen was trying to wake him. "Daddy, wake-up. Wake-up!" Since her voice couldn't do the trick, her hands would. She reached over and pinched his nose only to have his mouth fly open. She immediately covered that with her other hand and sure enough, Arthur gagged and awoke with a start.

"May I go to the mall with Ms. Beverley?"

"Ah, what, who?" replied Arthur, still disoriented.

"Ms. Beverley. She came back from Japan and is going shopping for Christmas presents and asked if I wanted to go. May I?"

Arthur sat up in his chair and instinctively wiped his face to clear his head. "Uhhhh, sure, go ahead," he said yawning. "But change your shirt and brush your teeth first, okay?"

"Thank you, daddy." She leaned in and kissed him on the cheek before sprinting up the stairs.

Arthur sat for a moment, reflecting on his waking dream. *It felt so real.* He leaned forward, bringing the recliner to a sitting position. In doing so, he faced the television directly and saw the broadcast of 'A Christmas Carol'. Glancing to his left, he focused on the remaining dregs of wine in a glass on the side table. The stem bled a red ring on its makeshift coaster, a newspaper article announcing the dates for an estate sale to liquidate the remaining assets of the late Ernest Bell. He chuckled at the obvious connection and in the time it took him to stand, stretch and yawn, his dream had faded like the ghost of Ernest Bell.

On his way into the kitchen he opened the side door leading to his driveway and dropped the newspaper into the recycle bin. The blast of cool air chased away any notion of dozing off again. He sauntered into the kitchen and placed the glass in the sink just as the doorbell rang. Expecting Beverley he shouted, "It's open," and peered into the foyer anticipating her entry.

Moments later it rang again. *Maybe it isn't Beverley.* He stepped into the foyer, stopping briefly to adjust the thermostat before opening the front door. Facing him through the storm doors' glass was the stunning image of Beverley, the glow of the overhead porch light bathing her in a soft cocoon of radiance.

Aware of his staring he tried to offset the intrusion by purposely fumbling with the lock on the storm door. Once opened, he held the door open as she stepped inside and greeted him with her usual playful acerbity.

"What took you so long? It's cold out there you know."

"I'm fine and how are you?"

They exchanged smiles and a casual hug. "Austen's upstairs getting ready, how was your flight?"

"My arms are tired, but other than that --"

"I keep setting you up, don't I?"

Beverley followed him into the kitchen, making sure to glance around the home for any signs of Christmas. The table in the foyer held a couple Christmas cards and half dozen scented candles in a bowl filled with sand, but other than that, nothing.

"No tree or decorations this year?"

"Didn't get around to it," he replied, re-corking the bottle of wine.

"That's what you said last year."

He intentionally ignored her as she took a seat at the island. "Do you want a glass?" he asked waving the bottle of wine seductively, enticing her to partake.

"No, thanks. You remind me of my Aunt Beatrice. But just the opposite."

"Yeah? How so?

"She never takes her Christmas tree down and you never put one up. She says that way, she's always ready for Christmas."

"And I'm always ready for it to be over. We both know how to stay ahead of the curve."

Beverley shrugged at the logic as he changed his mind and poured another glass of wine.

"I can't believe you're brave enough to go shopping on Christmas Eve."

"Why not? The stores aren't that crowded and you can get some pretty good deals."

"You'd get better deals if you wait until the day after Christmas," he goaded.

She leaned back, shook her head and made it a point to emphasizing each word, "You are such a Scrooge!"

"As I recall he owned his own business and didn't have a kid and a college fund to pay into," he reminded her.

Beverley considered carrying on the line of conversation, but thought better. She was not going to change him in a single sitting and they had had this discussion many times before. Instead, she turned her attention to a framed picture of Austen and her deceased mother, Camille, tacked to the refrigerator with a butterfly shaped magnet. Taken at the beach when Austen was two, both sat constructing a crude sand castle.

"They grow up so fast, don't they?"

"Six going on sixteen."

Beverley had always wanted to know the circumstances surrounding Camille's death, but never felt comfortable enough with their friendship to ask. Whenever she was with Austen and the issue of Camille came up, she would always withdraw, leaving Beverley to quickly change the subject.

Beverley was relieved when she heard the familiar clamor of tiny feet descending the stairs. Seconds later, Austen burst into the kitchen and announced, "I'm ready!"

"Come here," said Arthur putting down his glass of wine.

He inspected her face then picked her up and cradled her close.

"Now be a good girl and do daddy a huge favor."

"What?"

"Make sure you give Ms. Beverley a hard time. Okay?"

"I'll do my best," smiled Austen.

"I'm sure you will."

He kissed her on the cheek as he lowered her to the floor and shot Beverley a smug grin.

"I love you, daddy."

"I love you too, sweetheart."

Beverley knelt and made sure Austen's jacket was zipped

tight against her neck, and then held her hand.

"See you later, Arthur," she said sarcastically.

"Bye. Have a good time."

He followed them with his eyes as they exited the front door. A moment later, Beverley re-entered. "Why don't you come with us? It'll be fun."

Arthur thought about her offer for a moment, giving Beverley hope that he would accept. "Thanks, but you two go ahead and make it a girls' night out. And remember, whatever happens in the mall --"

"I know . . . stays in the mall."

Arthur took a sip of wine as she turned to leave. Like the wine on his tongue, he savored her beauty and allowed himself to entertain the thought of inviting another woman to share his life. Before exiting, she returned his stare and used a weak wave of her hand to ask him one last time to accompany her. His equally weak smile refused the invitation.

After she closed the door, he turned his gaze to the picture of Camille and Austen on the refrigerator door. It was as though he was expecting her to raise her head, tell him enough time had passed and grant him the blessing he needed to move on. However, her attention remained focused on Austen seated playfully between her outstretched legs, and his remained on Beverley.

CHAPTER 8

Claire usually received a phone call prompting her when Christmas Present was on his way to the office. This time, he took her by complete surprise when he backed in dragging two mailbags.

"What's all this?" She rushed to the door and held it open for him.

"Homework," he wheezed as he collapsed in his chair and then laid his head on the desk.

Claire grabbed a handful of letters and started sorting through them. "There must be a couple thousand letters here."

"Don't worry, there's more on the way."

"These are 'Urgent Reviews', what are we supposed to do with them?"

"I have to find a way to increase Christmas spirit in humans." He raised his head long enough to hand her Austen's letter before returning it to the desks top.

"Or?"

"Or we'll be cleaning the reindeer stables this time next

year."

"I see," said Claire finishing Austen's short letter, then folded and returned it to its envelope. "Looks like I need to book a flight south for the winter."

"Where are you going?" The thought of having to face this crisis without Claire's assistance quickly registered concern on his face.

"I'm not going anywhere. You are."

The look of concern now shifted to one of confusion. Claire dismissed both with a roll of her eyes and a deep sigh before crossing to the bookshelf.

"Visitations," she stated flatly while pulling a well-used tome from the shelf. "This isn't anything new, sir. It's like the yo-yo; every generation discovers it. Kids get frustrated, write a few letters; even though I must say I've never seen quite this many, and you end up making house calls . . . so to speak."

"What do you mean by house calls?"

She sighed once again. *Santa give me strength.* She stood in front of his desk and held the cover of the book for him to read.

"'A Christmas Carol' by Charles Dickens. Hey, I saw his picture in Santa's office," he said perking up.

"Its all right here, sir." She placed the book in front of him and opened it to a dog-eared page.

"I knew that name sounded familiar," he mumbled to himself.

"Gee, I wonder why?" remarked Claire sarcastically as she pointed to a highlighted set of paragraphs. On any other day, she would have left him to read in peace, but this was Christmas Eve and time was of the essence. After a few moments, she decided it best to offer a quick synopsis.

"Ebenezer Scrooge is a jerk who lacks Christmas spirit. You, the Ghost of Christmas Past and the Ghost of Christmas Future, visit him at his home and give the 'good ghost, bad ghost' routine. You as usual, play the good ghost. He's scared out of his wits, and by the time you leave, he understands why Christmas is a special time of the year," she summarized. "It's not all that complicated, sir,"

"Does it work?"

"Always," she said, and then added, "Well, at least it has so far."

She watched as he contemplated the thought. On cue, he quickly stood up and announced, "I like it! When can we start?"

She had to be careful. This needed to be his idea in order for him to have the necessary confidence to pull off his coming mission. "Well," she said coyly, "considering the time, you really should wait until after the new year. But, since it is Christmas Eve and in the book you make your visits the night *before* Christmas . . ." She paused as if thinking, giving him the time to interrupt her thoughts.

"I have an idea," he interjected as expected. "Let's do it tonight! That way Austen can change, enjoy Christmas Day, and I'll have some good news for Santa when he returns tomorrow morning."

"That's a great idea, sir. Wherever do you get them from?"

He smiled broadly at his plan and rubbed his hands together in anticipation. "What about Christmas Past and Christmas Future? Shouldn't we get together and work on a little game plan, you know, strategize, coordinate, synchronize our watches, that sort of stuff?"

"No," she stated flatly. "Christmas Past will know everything in a few minutes and the fact that we are talking about it now means that Christmas Future already knows. Trust me, they know what to do."

Claire left to let him start mulling over the thought of visiting humans. She felt a little guilty manipulating him in such an obvious manner, but it was her job. She knew how much he loved humans and suspected it was the reason Santa made him Director of Human Relations. As for her, she found humans ingratiating and erratic. They had a history of greed unheard of in the North Pole, but accepted as normal in their world. The Christmas season was supposed to appeal to their charitable nature, but over the decades, that sentiment had diminished and been replaced with the desire to accumulate and show off their wealth instead of sharing with the rest of humanity. None of it made any sense to her, but then again, she was not human.

Christmas Present however, was blissfully ignorant to their history and overlooked their petty foibles. He saw the good in humans and when the opportunity arose to engage them, relished in the thought that he could walk amongst them and share his optimism.

As she closed the door to his office, the joy he felt knowing that he was going to meet an actual child on Christmas Eve was more than he could stand. His emotions boiled over causing him to break out in song and dance. "I'm going to meet the humans, I'm going to meet the humans..."

CHAPTER 9

The Salvation Army Volunteer tried to shrug off the cold and pulled his coat tighter around his neck. The wind had died down, but now the temperature was dropping and his thin coat, earlier adequate to the task, was proving a liability. The sound of his bell carried far in the cool night air. For him, it was less a call for alms than it was a reason to keep moving, generate heat and keep warm. He contemplated leaving early, but the mall decided to keep their doors open late. Only a couple more hours and he could call it a night. After all, he had a duty to perform.

Most department stores closed at six o'clock on Christmas Eve, but with the economy in a recession and consumer confidence at an all time low, shoppers were looking more and spending less and stores knew it. Rather than get stuck with holiday inventory that would have to be liquidated at a loss after Christmas, the Mall's retailers slashed prices and stayed open late to appeal to last minute bargain hunters and delinquent shoppers.

This was precisely the reason the Salvation Army volunteer

held on and fought the cold. Hopefully, shoppers would be so pleased that they were able to find that last minute gift at a price unheard of three weeks ago they would show their appreciation with a sizable donation to his charitable cause as they exited the mall.

So far, his assessment had been correct. He had emptied his cash pot twice and thus, nearing the homestretch, he rang his bell with the fervor of a zealot, calling on all and thanking each in kind for their generosity.

Deep inside the bowels of the mall, Beverley also kept track of the time. With her list completed, all she had to do was pick up a few more rolls of wrapping paper and a package of bows. She had more than enough of both at the house, but her stockpile lacked the necessary variety for her taste. She did not like wrapping more than two gifts in the same pattern. It just seemed so cheap and easy.

She held the same sentiment for store wrapped gifts. Her purchases qualified her for free gift-wrapping and even though the staff of volunteers did a competent job, she never considered it an option. However, she made it a point to look at their displays for new ideas to try at home.

Satisfied with her choices, Beverley folded her list and pointed her gift-laden cart toward the mall entrance where she and Austen had entered. The mall was huge and Beverley silently cursed her decision to park at the entrance farthest from the bulk of her shopping. She had done so because she wanted to spend as much time with Austen as possible.

Afraid that Arthur's cavalier attitude toward Christmas was affecting Austen adversely, she wanted her to see the many

Christmas displays throughout the mall hoping they would awaken some passion for the season inside the stoic child. Maybe her plan had been too ambitious. Austen trailed unenthusiastically, but kept pace, leaving Beverley to wonder if she was tired, or just bored.

The mall loudspeaker crackled to life and announced they would be closing in fifteen minutes. The innocuous voice asked everyone to complete their shopping and begin making their way toward the exits. It clicked off, then as an afterthought, clicked on and wished everyone a 'Merry Christmas.'

Beverley still had half the mall to traverse. She stopped and rearranged the shopping bags in her cart to create a seat for Austen and lifted her into place. Austen immediately leaned forward, wrapped her arms around Beverley's neck and placed her head against her breast.

The tender sight evoked warm responses from passers by, but each kindhearted smile sent a wave of guilt cascading through Beverley. The source of her guilt sprang from the fact that she was not Austen's mother, yet complete strangers assumed she was and treated her as such.

Throughout the evening, in every store they had entered, staffers commented on how beautiful *her* daughter was, how well mannered *her* daughter was, and asked if *her* daughter was ready for Santa? One excessively flirtatious man went so far as to make the comparison, "In a few years, people will think you and *your daughter* are sisters."

Shame amplified her culpability. At first, she corrected the obvious error, which led to an apology and opened the door for a conversation about their real relationship. By the third engagement, she had simply responded with a 'thank you.' Now as she approached the Christmas Village located at the center of the mall, the deception gnawed at her.

To take her mind off the issue, she steered her cart into the Christmas tree forest to try to salvage the last part of her so far failed plan.

Brightly lit trees of every description surrounded them. The displays contained religious themes, children's toys, Christmas cards, holiday candy, ornate hand blown glass ornaments and winterscapes. Most were so laden with lights and garland the trees themselves were barely visible.

The tree that immediately caught Beverley's attention was the 'green' tree. Rooted in a large planter and decorated with dried flowers, pinecones and moss, it was destined for replanting after Christmas.

She opened her pitch with, "Austen, look at these Christmas trees, they are so beautiful. Which one do you like?"

"They're all pretty," said Austen, barely bothering to raise her head long enough for a full view.

So much for that, thought Beverley. *At least I tried*. She was about to leave when she noticed the mall's Santa seated on his ornate throne. A single child and his mother waited. Beverley stalled until the last child took his seat on Santa's lap, and then angled her cart toward Santa Claus' realm.

"Hey look Austen, Santa is still here. Why don't we take a picture with him before he heads back to the North Pole?"

Austen did not even bother to raise her head this time and stated flatly, "I don't want to."

"Awh, come on. There's no one in line. You can sit on his lap and tell him what you want for Christmas."

Taken aback by her silence, Beverley awaited her response.

Little does she know, I can be very persistent.

"How's he going to know what to bring you for Christmas if you don't go up there and tell him?"

Austen decided to put an end to this charade. She raised her head long enough to take a bored glance at the faux Santa. "He's not the real Santa Claus. I sent a letter to the real Santa two weeks ago. He already knows what I want."

Slightly embarrassed, Beverley could do little but smile and sigh at the candid revelation. A six year old had just unmasked her ruse, dismissed fiction with fact, destroyed her intention and rendered her speechless. As she pushed the cart toward the entrance, one thought crossed Beverley's mind. *People may think Austen is my daughter, but she's definitely Arthur's child.*

CHAPTER 10

With the end of his shift at hand, the Salvation Army Volunteer decided to finish with a flourish. Much to their delight, he showered the last stragglers exiting the mall with song by singing the lyrics to the canned instrumental Christmas music piped over the exterior speakers.

His impromptu plan worked well and brought the best kind of donations possible, silent ones; dollars instead of coins.

By the time Beverley and Austen appeared, he had just launched into, *It's The Most Wonderful Time of the Year.'*

Appreciative of the sentiment, she rewarded his efforts with a crisp ten-dollar bill. His heartfelt response, "God bless you and Merry Christmas," was followed with a sympathetic, "Awww," at the sight of Austen slumped against her chest.

"Merry Christmas to you too," replied Beverley for both she and Austen who was a picture of listless serenity at this point. By the time they reached the car, Beverley had to carry Austen to her seat and buckle her it. As she drove off, security guards were ushering the remaining customers from the mall and locking the doors behind them.

The Volunteer unhooked his cash pot, folded his stand and headed for the last car in the lot. The dilapidated wreck awaiting him doubled as both a home as well as needed transportation. After stowing his gear in the trunk he happily climbed inside the decaying vehicle, placed the cash pot in the passenger seat and turned over the engine. As he anxiously waited for the heat to kick in he reached behind the passenger seat for an insulated cooler hidden under a stack of old newspapers.

He sat the cooler on the floor of the passenger seat, pulled a beer from its icy depth and drank the frothy brew in one thirsty draw that elicited a wet belch. Pleased with himself, he crushed the can and placed it in a bag filled with other recyclables and then opened another as he gunned the engine and checked the vents for any sign of heat. Satisfied that warmth was on its way he pulled off his thin gloves and alternated holding his hands against the vent and blowing in them to warm his fingers. He noisily cracked his knuckles, checked the exterior mirrors to make sure he was alone, and then sat the cash pot in his lap. He greedily grabbed a wad of bills and smiled as he made a cursory accounting of the number of large denominations it contained.

He had already emptied the pot twice that night and this haul was shaping up to be the best. He made a mental note to learn the lyrics to as many Christmas standards as he could and start singing earlier next year. As for now he needed to leave the parking lot since Mall Security would be checking any remaining cars.

He sat the cash pot on the floor between his legs, took

another swig of beer and drove off to find a less conspicuous locale from which to count his many blessings.

Ten minutes later he pulled into and parked in an alley on the industrial side of the city. He knew the neighborhood well and was comfortable with this location. The company behind whose warehouse he now sat fired him for stealing less than two months ago.

As he carefully counted his cash, taking care to smooth and correctly orient each bill before placing them in their respective piles, he playfully tried to calculate how many hours he would have labored inside the warehouse to make as much money as he was now counting outside the warehouse.

The growing stacks of ill-gotten booty put him in a holiday mood. He turned on the radio and laughed at the serendipity. *'It's The Most Wonderful Time of the Year,'* was playing and as he sang along, continued to separate bills.

"It's the most wonderful time of the year!

With the kids jingle-belling and everyone telling you be of good cheeeeeer . . .

It's the most wonderful time of the year!"

Yes indeed, not only was it wonderful, it was profitable.

With his thoughts on his money and the radio providing the soundtrack to his criminal enterprise, the Volunteer paid no attention to the wind pick up in the alley.

The initial breeze lift papers from open dumpsters and chased loose dirt from its hiding place. His first indication of the coming storm should have been the cold draft whistling through the vents and cracks in his window's insulation but it was the sight of snow that eventually pricked his interest.

He stopped singing, turned off the radio and craned his neck forward to look skyward through the dirty windshield. Sporadic white flecks flew by as he wondered aloud, "Is it really starting to snow?"

It was cold but not that cold. No snowfall of any significance had fallen in Charleston since the freak snowstorm a couple months after Hurricane Hugo had roared through, yet there it was, being whipped by a wind that was intensifying with each passing second.

Had he a cleaner windshield and been more sober he would have realized the snowflakes were nothing more than Styrofoam packing peanuts. The walled confines of the alley had created a natural tunnel channeling the wind as it raged in a dusty vortex toward his car. Along the way it siphoned and scattered aloft the packing material from the dumpsters and stacked boxes left in its wake.

Suddenly, the buffeting wind was upon him and began to rock the car violently. Spooked by the elements, he leaped in his seat, upending the cash pot in his lap. In an attempt to save it, he banged his forehead on the steering wheel and began cursing his predicament.

Electromagnetic discharges from the whirlwind possessed the car's electrical system. The radio turned itself on and blared noisily as wiper blades flapped furiously against the windshield smearing the dirt and further obscuring his view. The overhead light began glowing bright. The emergency lights and headlights joined the chorus, as the horn trumpeted at will.

Terrified, he kicked open the door, rolled out and crawled for safety behind a sturdy dumpster. No sooner was he tucked safely behind the steel canister than the wind abruptly subsided. Other than the occasional leaf of paper descending, the alley drew silent as a grave.

He was about to peek out from his hiding place when he heard footsteps. He shrunk and turned his ear to listen for directional guidance. *Was it a cop? Probably not.* His past experiences with the law told him they would have identified themselves by now and called on him to come out. No, this had to be some underpaid security guard making his rounds.

The footsteps neared, then stopped.

He lay on the ground and peered out. From beneath the chassis of his car he could see two red stocking feet filling red pumps and breathed a sigh of relief. *A woman. Probably a prostitute looking for a trick.*

Rising to his feet, he climbed from behind the dumpster, looked inside his car to make sure his cash pot was intact and stepped into the alley to face the buxom, well-dressed woman. *A bit large for my taste, but then again, I am not a choosy man.* He had money to spend, might as well buy himself something nice for Christmas.

"Can I help you?" he asked seductively.

"Since you asked nicely, you may," she said coolly, then sprayed him with an atomized mist from a glass vial.

Initially the scent nearly gagged him. Afterwards it exploded into a cornucopia of Christmas flavors so rich he could almost taste them. His mind, racing to identify them all, forced his senses into overdrive. The intoxicating rush of adrenaline was so powerful it sent him reeling in every direction at once like a tailless kite in a windstorm.

It was an experience only the irrational mind could describe. He saw Ezekiel's wheel in the sky, piloted Einstein's beam of light and climbed Jacob's ladder. It was the reason dogs chased their tails and had he one would have done the same.

Laughing like a giddy child on a mental roller coaster, he staggered drunk through the alley babbling in languages previously unknown to mankind, yet clearly understood by him to be his own.

The euphoria finally consumed him. He sank to his knees with arms outstretched grasping for salvation, a repentant sinner at confessional thanking humanity for the chance to atone for the wasted life he had led.

He slowly opened his eyes and in his delusionary state could see them clearly; the spirits of all he had wronged throughout the years, robbing them of the charity freely given.

He leapt to his feet, ran to his car and began stuffing the neatly ordered piles of cash into the pot. Careful to scoop up the spilled money on the floorboard, he even gathered the loose coins in the ashtrays and glove compartment before burrowing like a madman between the seat cushions for any hidden monies. Satisfied that he had everything, he rushed back into the alley.

They spirits seemed so shy hiding in the shadows around him. He held out his hand showing them the money and assured them it was all right. He tossed coins like a benched retiree feeding pigeons, coaxing them to come forward to receive their portion. And come they did.

They issued forth in waves from below and above and surrounded him. Like candy at Halloween, he handed out money until it was all gone, yet they continued to come and pressed him for more. Their faces, once full of compassion, twisted into hideous shapes and transformed into masks of greed. He screamed as they overwhelmed him, tearing at his clothes for more and ripping into his flesh for their share.

The woman looked on with annoyance as the volunteer spun in every direction. She breathed deeply, shook her head in disgust and forced an exasperated sigh as he screamed and tore the flesh from his own body until he lay dying in a pool of blood harvested by his own hands.

Moments later the wind began to rise as before. Once white, the Styrofoam snow filling the alley sky was tainted with blood and mixed with bills of every denomination drifting downward as the wind subsided.

Like a punch line to a bad joke, the only sound in the alley came from the car radio playing, *'Let it Snow, Let it Snow, Let it Snow.'*

CHAPTER 11

The sight of Beverley cradling a sleeping Austen greeted Arthur. She looked so peaceful he was almost tempted to point Beverley upstairs and let her put his little angel to bed.

"Awwww, you tired my little angel out," he said stepping outside to initiate the gentle transfer.

"I think we tired each other out," replied Beverley completing the transaction.

He glanced over Beverley's shoulder and saw the back seat of her car piled high with shopping bags. "I see you did your patriotic best to help stimulate the economy. You need a hand?"

"I'll manage. Yours are somewhat full right now. But if you feel like helping me gift wrap --"

"Whoa, look at the time," interrupted Arthur. "I better get this girl to bed. It's way past her bedtime."

Beverley smiled and stroked Austen's back lovingly. She had a long night ahead of her and though tired was looking forward to it.

"Merry Christmas, Arthur."

"You too, Bev."

"You too, what?" she exacted, striking a challenging pose.

Arthur smiled and shook his head at her persistence. "Season's Greetings, Happy Holidays, Happy Hanukkah, Happy Kwanzaa, Merry Christmas and a Happy New Year," then sang, "and many moooorrrre, Beverley!" to punctuate his retort.

Backing away, she laughed at his holiday humor and shot back, "You too, Arthur."

As expected, Austen showed little sign of waking as Arthur took off her clothes and put on her pajamas. He pulled back her covers and laid her on her back, then waited patiently for her to instinctively roll onto her stomach and settle in before adjusting her covers. Moments later the sound of her breathing told him she was falling deeper into sleep.

The digital clock sitting on the nightstand next to the bed flipped its time to 9:53. Next to it stood a framed picture of Austen and Camille. He picked it up gently, angling it slightly so the glow of the streetlight casting shadows in the room could illuminate the image. Tears welled in his eyes as he kissed his finger and brushed it over Camille's face leaving a slight smudge. He wiped it clean with the sleeve of his sweatshirt and quietly set the photo back in place.

Arthur studied Austen's peaceful face as she slept. He stroked her hair lightly, secured the covers closer around her neck and straightened the twisted sleeve of her pajama top on her exposed arm, smiling as she twitched slightly under his care. He held her tiny fist in his hand, stretched out her fingers and marveled at their delicate detail. Her fist closed around his forefinger and he could feel her measured pulse as her palm contracted with every breath she took.

Before he was married he could not imagine having children and being a father. Now as he looked at Austen sleeping peacefully he could not imagine life without her. Once again tears welled in his eyes as he pulled free his finger. Leaning forward, he placed a kiss on her cheek and whispered softly in her ear, "I love you. It's just you and me now kid."

He got up, crept toward the door, exited, then poked his head back in and added softly, "Merry Christmas, sweetheart."

Beverley was not the only one who had a long night ahead. Arthur had purchased a bicycle for Austen and needed to assemble it. He should have let the store do it, but fearful of having a proper place to hide it, he had decided to assemble it himself and had hid the nondescript cardboard box in the crawl space under the back deck.

He was not adept with tools, but the salesclerk had assured him assembly was a simple task considering he only had to attach the wheels, chain, and tighten the handlebars. The necessary tools and instructions were included in the accompanying kit.

He would wait a couple hours, then accomplish his mission and leave the bicycle sitting in the living room along with the helmet for her to discover in the morning. After breakfast he would take her to Hampton Park and let her ride.

Whatever guilt he felt earlier about any romantic thoughts

for Beverley was released under the cascade of hot water massaging the back of his neck. Though the bathroom filled with steam to the point he could barley see his hand in front of his face, he remained steadfast under the nozzle until the water began to cool.

After drying off he wrapped the towel around his waste, wiped the steam from the mirror with the palm of his hand and recoiled at the reflection. It was none other than the face of Ernest Anthony Bell III staring back at him.

"Omigod! The ghost from my dream!"

"The very same soul," replied Ernest in an eerily hollow voice.

Arthur couldn't believe it. He quickly retreated to the safety of the shower stall on weakening legs and fought to regain his footing along with his composure. After a few moments, he peeped out and seeing nothing, mustered the courage to edge forward and peek around the edge of the mirror as if foolishly trying to creep up on his own shadow. Once there, he came face to face with his own reflection. Ernest was gone.

"I must be dreaming again," he muttered to himself.

"You still don't believe in me, do you?" came the voice from behind him. Arthur spun on the moist tiles and fell away from the sight of the mist shrouded Spirit now standing in front of him.

He crumbled to the floor and scrambled to make himself smaller against the clothes hamper in the corner of the bathroom. His action only served to enrage the frustrated spirit.

Ernest angrily gathered his length of chains with a swoop of his spindly arm, raised them high and in a show of force clanged them loudly as he screamed in a voice so shrill that had Arthur been born deaf his very soul would have heard it.

"*Spiritless fool! Do you or don't you believe I am here?*" shrieked Ernest.

"Yes! Yes! I do, I do, I do. I believe! You're real!" cried Arthur from beneath the towel shielding his face.

"*Then open your eyes and look at me!*" demanded the spirit from beyond the grave. He initiated another wail that raised the hairs on Arthur's head and began swinging the length of chains wildly; the iron links and crude cash boxes sparked against the ceramic tiles with each pass. Shredded chunks of wood and plaster were ripped from the walls and door and flew about the bathroom in the ghostly maelstrom.

Terrified by the onslaught, Arthur scrambled behind the freestanding claw foot tub just as the bathroom mirror and shower enclosure shattered, raining shards of glass into the tub and throughout the small space. The toilet roll shot streams of paper skyward and every bottle containing fluid burst, splattering the walls and ceiling with color. The assault left Arthur hyperventilating with fear.

Ernest finally drew quiet. He took a seat on the hamper. His transparent face, once angry, softened into a mask of remorse as he surveyed the totality of his destruction.

"*Listen to me for I must be on my way. Listen!*" he pleaded softly.

Arthur peeked out over the edge of the tub. Seeing the pained look on Ernest's face he found himself feeling sorry for the ghost and slowly emerged from his hiding spot. He took a seat on the edge of the bathtub and faced the forlorn Spirit. "I'm listening," he whispered.

Ernest extended his arm, eerily closing the distance between the two and pointed a spindly finger at Arthur, nearly touching him.

"I am here to warn you, Arthur Fisher. This is your only chance of escaping my fate. You will be visited tonight."

Like Scrooge, the revelation shook Arthur to his core. "What? Tonight!"

"The come to turn you from the path I once freely walked."

"Who?'" interrupted Arthur indignantly. "Who's coming?"

A flash of fear crossed Ernest's face. Arthur flinched as the he abruptly stood and began to wrap his chains around his arm, gathering them for his eternal journey.

"I can tell you no more than they arrive from distant regions." He cocked his head slightly as if hearing a remote voice. *"I must leave now. I'm not allowed to rest or loiter, but compelled to walk the earth for eternity. It is my penance for a wasted life. As for you, they will come as they came for me at the eleventh hour."*

"Who? Who's coming at eleven?"

"I can say no more," replied Ernest, and then turned to leave.

"Wait a minute," shouted Arthur in an exasperated voice. "Are these supposed to be the same fairy tale Christmas ghosts that visited Scrooge? That was a book, none of that was real!"

Arthur stood up and reached for Ernest's shoulder in a bid to delay his departure. "Wait a minute!" he demanded as his hand swept through the transparent body.

Arthur felt a lump in his throat when Ernest stopped in his tracks. He began turning without actually spinning his body. Arthur swallowed hard as he seemed to fold inward until a nose and a pair of eyes slowly emerged from the back of his head. The temperature in the bathroom began to drop as his face and eventually his whole body inverted. Arthur looked to see if an open window was allowing for the invading draft then suddenly realized it was Ernest. His features, once translucent, were now opaque and pallid, giving credence to the seriousness of his pending warning. He drifted close enough for Arthur to smell his frosty breath, had he one.

"Listen to me, Arthur Fisher! For your sake listen and remember what I have said. Your existence as well as the fate of your child rests in the balance." With that Ernest began to fade. He kept his eyes on Arthur as he backed through the bathroom door. Arthur could feel his heart pounding in his chest as the ghostly chains snaked past his feet following their owner into the mist.

Waiting to make sure Ernest was gone for good, Arthur sat on the edge of the tub, closed his eyes and held his head in his hands trying to come to grips with what he had just witnessed. *Was this just another dream?* When he opened his eyes the bathroom had returned to its original pristine state before Ernest's arrival; complete with the cloud of steam still hanging in the air. The sight of the eerie mist spooked him, causing him to unconsciously bite his nails, something he had not done since he was Austen's age.

Austen!

He quickly stepped into his pants and ran out the bathroom. She had to have heard the racket and was probably wondering what was going on. Chances were she did as he had always instructed her to do if any emergency arose; lock herself in her room and dial 9-1-1.

He could see it now: police arriving at any minute and he trying to explain to them how the noise had been created by an angry ghost that had stopped by to warn him a trio of spirits were on their way.

Her door was as he left it, slightly ajar, the lights off. He opened it slightly and peered inside her room. She was still sleeping fitfully. He glanced at her clock. 10:25. 'Whatever it was' would arrive in 35 minutes.

He eased shut her door and bolted for his bedroom. *Think, Arthur, think!* Why was this happening to him? According to Ernest this was all about Austen. His observation was true. When it came to Christmas, admittedly, Arthur was not the most observant father. That had been Camille's forte. She was the one that had enjoyed the season and everything that came with it.

Each year there had to be a different exterior display. Like a field general she would direct as he stood for hours in the cold, testing, then stringing lights and carefully placing lawn displays in ever changing formations to meet her specific demands.

Only when the exterior was finished was she ready for the tree. Finding the 'perfect' tree was an evolution unto itself. Each year he had to take her to at least three different lots before she would settle on the right one. Once home, the tree had to stand straight as an arrow, then trimmed further to assure its symmetry. He once made the mistake of suggesting they buy an artificial tree and nearly paid for it with his life.

Inside their home 'fresh' garland created from the trimmings of the Frazier Fir were bundled and wrapped with bows then tied to the stair handrail. The remaining branches found a home elsewhere on the mantle, tables and bookshelves.

Sand filled bowls played host to candles of all sizes with seasonal scents and cinnamon scented pinecones. Christmas cards were treasured keepsakes and found a place on every horizontal surface and even the Christmas tree.

Then there was the music. In Camille's household only Christmas music was allowed between Thanksgiving and the New Year.

Throughout the years she had amassed an impressive collection of antique glass ornaments. She would unwrap each, polish, and then affix them to the tree with new hardware each year. He loved watching her and would sit back and relax with a cup of hot cocoa and eventually drift off to sleep next to the fire while she meticulously decorated the tree. The only other person he had met that had as much Christmas spirit was Beverley.

Beverley! The thought of salvation pulled him to his feet. If there was anyone who could strengthen any lack of recognition he had for the season it was she. If these so called spirits did show up, who better to argue his case than Beverley? She would be his star witness of sorts. Was this some bad dream or a guilt-laden manifestation, as he suspected, they would just enjoy each other's company and have a great time together.

He grabbed his watch and glanced at the time. 10:33. He had to hurry! Racing to get dressed, his mind ran through a series of scenarios. How could he convince Beverley that he needed to spend some time with her without seeming too obvious and alerting her to his dilemma? He certainly could not explain it to her. She would not believe him and if nothing happened he would have to hear about it everyday as long as they were neighbors.

He checked his appearance in the mirror then sprinted down the stairs two steps at a time. He ran to the closet in the downstairs guest bedroom and found what he was looking for; some left over rolls of wrapping paper and a bag of bows with labels.

He dashed into the kitchen and glanced at the time on the microwave clock. 10:40. Throwing open the cabinets, he grabbed a pitcher and filled it with eggnog. The furious activity made him sweat and threatened to expose his plan before he had a chance to set it in motion. He wiped his face with a dishrag and then opened the freezer door and stuck his face inside to cool off further. He placed his hands, still shaking uncontrollably, on his thighs to steady them but the shakes transferred to his legs.

Realizing he would never be ready and wasting time, he gathered his load and headed next door.

Standing outside Beverley's door, the cold night air accomplished what the freezer could not and helped him concentrate as he ran through his prepared text. He checked the time again: 10:43. *Good.* That would give him enough time to get inside and wrap a couple gifts before anything was supposed to happen.

He took a deep breath and rang the doorbell. The chime reverberated with a Christmas theme and proved his decision correct. *I'm in the right place.*

"Who is it?" Beverley's tentative voice seeped through the door.

"It's me, Arthur, from next door," he reassured her.

"Arthur?" He could hear the concern in her voice. "Hold

on."

He hid his possessions behind his back. She opened the door quickly and immediately searched his eyes for any sign of the trouble that would have brought him to her door this time of night. His coy smile put her at ease, leaving her to decipher the mystery it held.

"Hey, what's up?"

"Uhhh, nothing," he shrugged. "Austen's sleeping, reruns on TV, soooooo," the longer he drew out the syllable, the broader her smile widened. "I decided to take you up on your offer to help wrap gifts."

He pulled the hand holding the rolls of wrapping paper from behind his back and waved them in her face like a child taunting a playmate with the latest new toy.

"Ooooh, he brought his private stash," she replied with an impressed look.

Basking in her approval, he relished the look men are given by women who decide to exercise their prerogative to re-evaluate friends through lovers eyes if they have reason to believe they may have overlooked something.

"Drinks, too," he added, pulling the pitcher from its hiding spot. He needed her to accept his attempt at companionship without question but did not expect his ruse to work quite as well as it did. She opened the door wide and grabbed him by his collar.

"You better get your butt in here before Santa's sleigh falls out the sky and kills you."

CHAPTER 12

With less than two hours to go before Christmas, instead of preparing for his visit with Austen, the Ghost of Christmas Present found himself walking briskly through the cavernous facility known to all as 'Gift Wrapping'. Despite Claire's warnings against it, he wanted to personally inform Santa that he had come up with a plan to combat the rising tide of dissatisfied letters and was not only executing it that very night, but would also have a full progress report awaiting him on his return.

It was crunch time in the North Pole and nowhere was more reflecting of that than Gift Wrapping. The facility was a hive of activity. At every turn, Elves dressed in green one-piece utility suits, hard hats and safety glasses operated and monitored a maze of machinery whose sole function was to ensure the smooth processing and loading of gifts on the sleigh. To say it ran like clockwork would have been an insult to elfin technology. The streamlined efficiency was the byproduct of decades of evolution and forward thinking on the part of many.

Every detail was addressed then audited by an oversight committee who continuously reviewed and analyzed ways to increase productivity while adhering to the strict quality control code demanded by Santa.

The staff at Gift Control generated the necessary request certificates based on children's performance evaluations. Though the age-old assessment of whether a child was 'Naughty' or 'Nice' remained the determining factor, the Awards Committee also considered whether the gift requested was consistent with their particular need before any award could be authorized. After all, children were impractical by nature and often times made requests that were well beyond their or their parents' means to handle. A child's safety was of paramount concern. Gifts like ponies (a favorite amongst little girls, and real race cars for boys), were always denied and replaced with more suitable alternatives.

Once approved, Gift Coordinators working the main floor received the request orders and passed them along to teams of Inventory Control Specialists under their supervision. Their jobs were to retrieve gifts from the various storerooms beneath the facility and bring them to the main floor for further processing. Sensors scanned the gifts' dimensions, calculated the volume and selected the appropriate shipping box. Automated arms assembled and filled each box with packing material, placed the gift inside, then sealed the box. After that they were seamlessly gift wrapped, fitted with color coordinated ribbons and bows, then hand written tags were applied to give the gift a touch of warmth.

Millions of gifts had to be stowed on Santa's sleigh and the 'Transformation' chamber took care of that. Christmas

Present tried to watch the final process, but a Supervisor respectfully asked he move along. He would have seen nothing either way since the unit was completely sealed. Had he been able to see inside, he would have witnessed a gift molecularly disassembled into phased matter. The resulting energy stream was buffered and streamed into massive hard drives on the sleigh where they awaited reanimation moments before delivery.

Christmas Present marveled at the technology as he strode confidently toward the sleigh where he knew he would find Santa. He hardly needed directions since the massive vehicle rest on a raised platform and was visible from every location in the facility.

Though he could not remember, he had ridden in the sleigh many times. Like everything thing else about the North Pole, it was spectacular. Humans still held with the nostalgic image of Santa Claus riding in an open cart of varied design depending on the artist's depiction and pulled by a team of reindeer. It may have been true in earlier days but with the exponential growth of Christmas over the past century, a wooden sleigh was no only impractical, it was downright ridiculous.

As he approached the sleigh Christmas Present slowed and stared with awe as though seeing it for the first time. Considering his condition, it literally was. It was a massive aircraft that resembled the Space Shuttle in overall design. The detailed Yule embellishments and insignia gave it the necessary aesthetic value to pay homage to its humble beginnings while conforming to the aerodynamic needs of a craft larger than an Air Force cargo plane.

It was rumored to be the inspiration for the Space Shuttle

after NASA analyzed a top-secret photo taken by an orbiting spy satellite that inadvertently captured a blurred and grainy image of the sleigh during its first shakedown flight. To meet with future needs, construction on a new sleigh had begun, but it would not be operational for another 24 months. Though old by their standards, the current sleigh still performed its mission adequately. Its technology and operational parameters were far beyond anything humans even considered aeronautically feasible and would not discover until the next quarter century had passed.

After taking in his fill of the sleigh, Christmas Present delved into the swarm of technicians and auxiliary men to find Santa inspecting the exterior with Sebastian, the Maintenance Supervisor.

"I had diagnostics run on the defroster like you asked, sir," informed Sebastian while wiping his grease stained hands with an equally greasy rag. "We didn't find anything out of spec but I had the heating coil replaced just to be on the safe side."

"Did you find what was causing that little scraping noise I heard somewhere over here on the left side?" pointed Santa.

"A worn bushing, sir. We replaced it and lubed the springs. She should run quieter now, sir."

"Thank you, Sebastian. Do me a favor and tell Oliver I need to see the weather report."

"Yes sir."

Seeing his opportunity to have a word with Santa, Christmas Present straightened his tie and approached.

"What is it Christmas Present?" asked Santa while continuing his walk-through.

"Well sir, after our meeting this morning, I did some

research and decided that the best way to deal with this --"

"You requested the weather report, sir?" interrupted Oliver, the Meteorologist. He seemed to come out of nowhere to hand Santa his leather bound binder of forecast predictions.

"Excellent!" replied Santa.

"That's the complete real time forecast as of two minutes ago. The one, three, six and twelve hour projections are color coordinated on the overlays, sir."

As Christmas Present waited patiently, Santa thumbed through the pile of colorful charts laid out by continent.

"Any areas of concern for tonight?"

"A couple of hot spots, sir. A wicked nor'easter is due to hit New England just after your arrival, blizzard conditions in varied parts of Northern Europe and a rather severe low pressure system is dumping heavy rains along the Chilean coast."

"El Nino, huh?" surmised Santa with a concerned ruffle of his brow.

"Yes sir," replied Oliver. "We're continuing to update the models and will have the current forecast estimates uploaded before departure. Other than that, you should have a smooth flight."

"Thanks, Oliver," sighed Santa. He initialed the report then turned to address Christmas Present. "What were you saying, Present?"

"Uh...ahh...I'm sorry, sir. I forgot what I was going to say."

CHAPTER 13

Beverley's home was as cozy and inviting as Arthur had imagined. The Christmas music, decorations, tree, and roaring fireplace temporarily transported him into a home inhabited by Camille.

The layout of Beverley's side of the duplex was the same as Arthur's, just opposite. In the three years she had been his neighbor, he had been inside her home many times, but only as far as the foyer when he came to pick up Austen. She had volunteered to babysit a month after moving in. He assumed she was just being nice since he had helped her carry some boxes when she was moving in, but her invitation had persisted and he soon accepted.

She proved to be a blessing in disguise. When Austen started day care he had difficulty coordinating his working hours around picking her up, but with Beverley's flexible hours and extended days off, she would often pick up Austen for him and care for her until he got home. Since she refused to accept any money for her services, he showed his gratitude by making it a point to keep her side of the yard cut and landscaped.

Over the years their friendship had blossomed into one of trust and respect. He was aware of a couple men she had dated, but neither relationship seemed to have legs which made him wonder why such a smart and beautiful woman with a biting wit couldn't find a special someone to share her life. Maybe that was the problem. She was too smart and too beautiful. Successful women who had their heads screwed on tight always seemed to have a hard time finding men, especially men willing to wait around long enough to get to know them before attempting exploration of other areas of their personality.

There was no doubt he was attracted to her, but her close proximity negated any chance of a romantic relationship. She might as well have been a co-worker as far as he was concerned. If he made a move and the relationship did not work out, the last thing he wanted was to have a neighbor he loathed seeing on a daily basis. It was best they remain friends.

Arthur sat cross-legged on the floor across from Beverley in the living room with his back to the fireplace trying his best to wrap a gift. He could tell by Beverley's stolen glances that his attempt was falling short of her expectations, but he stubbornly carried on in an effort to maintain his ruse long enough so as not to raise any suspicions surrounding his unexpected visit.

After wrestling with the ribbon, he patted a bow on the crudely wrapped gift and proudly handed it to her for labeling. She inspected it and offered a forced smile of approval that told him it would be rewrapped after he left. When she turned to set it aside, quarantining it from the other neatly wrapped gifts, he stole a glance at his watch. 10:56.

"You keep checking the time," she noticed. "If you need to leave . . ."

"No, no, no, I'm fine," he interrupted. "I'm just keeping track since I left Austen by herself."

"Maybe you should go check on her," she suggested with real concern.

"I've only been over here for fifteen minutes. Tell you what, I'll wrap one more gift, then I'll go."

"I don't know," she said referring to his previous attempt, "Maybe that's a sign you should leave now."

"Heyyyyy, be nice. I haven't done this in awhile," defended Arthur.

He purposely picked up his glass of eggnog with his left hand and stole another glance at his watch. 10:58. Two more minutes until the spirits were supposed to arrive. After taking a sip and setting the glass down, he felt his hands begin to tingle, and then shake. Under the guise of warming them, he rubbed his hands together and swiveled around to face the fire. With Beverley seated strategically behind him, the move placed him in a position to glance sidelong into the other rooms for any sign of movement. His last encounter with Ernest taught him that spirits had the ability to appear at any place or time of their choosing.

If he thought his act was proceeding smoothly, it was not. Beverley was hardly convinced and secretly blamed herself for his inability to relax. This was the first time they had been in such an intimate setting and quite frankly it had all the markings of an impromptu date. She was equally as nervous but was able to mask her uneasiness by concentrating on the gift she was wrapping.

Beverley appeared grateful for the sound of the wind picking up. It cut the uncomfortable silence and gave her something to react to. As for Arthur, the timing of the unexpected disturbance was too coincidental and in his mind heralded the encounter foretold by Ernest.

"Wow, where'd that come from?" questioned Beverley as she rose to investigate the weather. Arthur looked at his watch. 11:00. He leaped to his feet and tried to restrain his growing fear as the gale stiffened and began to howl. He quickly stepped over the coffee table and joined Beverley standing at the window peering through the blinds.

"Man, it's really blowing out there," observed Beverley, "must be a storm on the way." Arthur was too busy performing a continuous scan of every wall including the ceiling throughout the apartment for any sign of a spirit to hear her. The sound of a chair skidding across the porch sent shivers down his spine.

"What was that?" he whispered conspiratorially. Without thinking, he edged closer to Beverley and hugged her waist as he lifted open another slat on the blind and peered out. "Did you hear that?"

The feel of his arm around her waist surprised Beverley. She shifted and seeing the fearful look on his face mistook it for embarrassment. He quickly released her and forced a timid smile.

"Kind of jumpy aren't you?" She closed the slat and turned to face him. "It's just the wind. It knocked over some stuff on the porch."

They were standing close enough to kiss. She placed her hand against his chest as she eased past and could feel his heart racing. *Am I causing this?* "I'll be right back."

It was now 11:01 and the wind was subsiding. *Maybe the Spirit is waiting for her to leave before appearing.* If so, he would not grant it the opportunity it needed to catch him alone. Besides, his watch may have been running a bit slow and any extra time he could waste would be to his advantage.

"I'll give you a hand," he added quickly and rushed to open the front door and lead the way before she had a chance to respond.

By 11:05, they had finished straightening up the porch and returned inside. Arthur took comfort in believing that ghosts were supposed to be punctual by nature.

"Thanks for the help," said Beverley.

"Don't thank me until you've seen the bill," he said closing the door behind her.

"Maybe you should go and check on Austen." It was more a question than a statement. He looked at his watch, 11:06. *There's no ghost coming.* He was sure of that. Moreover, even if they were there, Beverley's presence was keeping them at bay. Why tempt fate? Best he remain where he was just in case.

"Nah, I'm sure she's okay. I would hate to wake her. She may not want to go back to sleep."

"I know I wouldn't," said Beverley. She turned and headed for the kitchen, asking, "You want some more eggnog?"

"Sure, why not?" Arthur's mood had changed dramatically. With the growing realization that his encounter with Ernest was . . . he didn't know what it was, but accepted it as some kind of waking dream brought on by the stress he was prone to feeling during the holiday season. Whatever the cause, knowing that it was over, he suddenly felt relaxed and able to enjoy

Beverley's company. *Who knows, maybe I'll try my hand at wrapping another gift.*

"Do you have any rum to spice up the eggnog?" he asked joining her in the kitchen.

"I thought you'd never ask. There's a bottle in that cabinet," she said pointing behind him.

As Beverley disappeared in the living room to retrieve their glasses, he opened the bottle of rum, inhaled the warm scent of butter and spice and thought, "ghosts . . . pfft, yeah right."

CHAPTER 14

Austen stirred under the covers. Though Arthur had covered her with the comforter, her body felt a draft chilling her shoulder and feet. In an involuntary reaction to the creeping cold, she reached for the quilt lying across the foot of her bed. Her unconscious mind, usually capable of protecting the body against such minor shifts without completely waking the mind, needed some help. The quilt was not there.

Austen slowly awoke and found she was lying on a cold stone surface. She sat up and rubbed her eyes, helping them adjust to the dark room slightly illuminated by a few beams of fluorescent light shining down from the grates high above on the far wall. She looked around the room to gain a sense of where she was and then grew wide eyed at the sight of a woman standing a few feet away staring at her.

She was a large woman, even by human standards. Dressed in all red with a spattering of green and white accessories, her voluptuous frame stood like an edifice to femininity firmly anchored by two pillars she called legs. Her face displayed the wisdom of centuries past and reduced to folly anyone with the courage to stare into it. Glaring down at the confused child, she managed to produce a disingenuous smile, which served to soften a perennially stern face.

"Hello Austen."

"Hello. Who are you?"

"I am the Ghost of Christmas Past," she answered stepping closer.

Austen should have been scared but the woman's beguiling smile and non-threatening posture momentarily eased her concerns. It did not help that Austen's favorite movie was the Wizard of Oz and like Dorothy, she imagined herself part of some adventurous dream.

"Where am I?' she asked standing up and brushing the dirt from her pajamas.

"You're at the North Pole. Santa Claus read your letter and wanted to meet you."

Austen's jaw dropped open at the revelation.

"He's really real!" she screeched.

"Of course he is," said Christmas Past with a genuine smile. "And he wants you to see he's real."

Austen looked around at the drab storeroom filled with cardboard boxes. If this were the North Pole, where were the snowmen, elves and reindeer? Dorothy had arrived in the colorful Oz to a welcoming chorus of Munchkins. She had flown there in a house with the help of a violent cyclone. Austen tried as best she could to remember how she had arrived at her present drab location, but her mind drew a blank.

"How did I get here?"

"The Ghost of Christmas Future came to your house and picked you up while you were sleeping."

"Is my daddy here too?"

"No. He's still at home."

Oh no. This would not do. North Pole or no North Pole, from the time she could remember, her father had drummed into her head that she was never to go anywhere without telling him, and certainly never with a stranger. The smile on the woman's face seemed friendly enough, but something was not right. She slowly backed away from Christmas Past, growing fearful with each step.

"I'm not supposed to talk to strangers or go anywhere with them without my daddy knowing," she said warily, looking for a place to run or hide.

Throughout the ages, there were learned men who could barely stand to rationalize or debate with the Ghost of Christmas Past. She was a walking textbook, a storehouse of all knowledge. The entire collection of the Library of Congress was little more than a short story to her. A six-year-old girl, regardless of how clever she may have been for her age, did not stand a chance.

"But I'm not a stranger, Austen," she smoothly intoned while closing the distance between them. Her face further softened and seemed to take on the appearance of a trusted grandmother approaching her granddaughter. As she stared into her eyes, Austen could almost smell the scent of fresh-baked cookies.

"I work with Santa Claus. He is a close friend and wants to be yours as well. Since I know *your* name and you know mine, that makes us friends because strangers don't know each other's names, do they?"

"No, ma'am," replied Austen in a trusting voice.

"That's right Austen they don't. If I weren't a friend, how would I know where you lived? Would Santa Claus let a stranger read the letter you wrote him? The one you labeled 'For Santa Claus Only'."

"No, ma'am."

"That's right, he wouldn't. So we must be friends, right?"

"I guess so," rationalized Austen.

"Of course we are," said Christmas Past softly as she reached out to take Austen's hand in hers. "Come on, I'll take you to meet him."

"You're going to take me to meet the real Santa Claus."

"Yes, but first we need to make a little stop and see another friend of ours. Okay?"

"Okay," agreed Austen. A bright smile graced her face as she happily followed the Ghost of Christmas Past through the storeroom's large oak door and into a dark corridor toward her unimagined destiny.

Having abandoned all pretenses, Arthur was content to slouch lazily in front of the fire and watch Beverley continue to painstakingly wrap gifts. He could not decide whether she had been a tailor or a surgeon in another life. Her expertise in cutting wrapping paper to meet the exact dimensions of each gift with the minimum of waste baffled him. Her nimble fingers folded each seam with meticulous care and joined the corners with mathematical precision. Any gift not meeting her approval was unwrapped immediately without hesitation.

"Why do you have to wrap your gifts so perfectly?"

"Because I care," she said after inspecting the latest gift for any sign of flaw. "I care about the person I'm giving it to."

"It doesn't bother you that they're going to rip all your caring up in about three seconds."

"Nope. I want them to," she said smugly.

After scratching the name off her master list she reached for another gift and studied which roll of wrapping paper to use. The snicker on Arthur's pursed lips questioned her reasoning.

"They do that because they're excited," she explained while measuring out the correct amount of paper. "Which means they care as much about getting the gift as I did giving it."

Correction; she was a lawyer in her past life.

"You always win, don't you?"

"Yep," she replied with a satisfied grin. She took a swig of eggnog and savored the added flavor of rum and the pinch of nutmeg and cinnamon added to enhance the flavor.

Arthur turned his attention toward the fire. Much like him, its intensity had mellowed and now burned lazily on settled logs. It seemed to sense his need for solemn reflection and did its best to provide him with a palette of slow moving flames designed to hypnotize his conscious mind and allow his subconscious the room necessary to contemplate the day's happenings. Beverley watched the flames glow reflect off the side of his face and for the first time since she had known him, he seemed without a care in the world. She wondered what he was thinking.

"You seem relaxed. You were kind of jumpy earlier."

"That's just the rum kicking in," he replied in a distant voice.

She could see he had something on his mind, but did not know how to ask. In the past, their conversations were cordial but rarely ventured past the topic of Austen, their jobs, or the customary 'how was the weekend'? On certain occasions when he was dropping Austen off for her to watch he would offer a bit more out of obligation but both knew she would always tell him an explanation was unnecessary. It was their routine and each abided by the unspoken rules of the game.

She decided not to push it. The fact that he was even sitting there was possibly a sign that their friendship was ready for more substantial dialogue based on mutual interest rather than proximity.

It was almost as if he were reading her mind. He suddenly turned away from the fire, sat up and faced her across the coffee table. The suddenness of his movement and the look on his face intrigued her. Whatever he was about to reveal had been brewing for a long time. His eyes narrowed as though searching for the correct way to phrase his thoughts.

"Have you ever . . . you ever have one of those dreams that was so real you thought you were awake?"

Taken aback by the abruptness of his question, Beverley deflected her confusion with humor.

"Are you about to tell me you wet the bed?"

"I keep setting you up, don't I? That was a gift, Merry Christmas," he mused, and then shifted back to a more thoughtful gaze. "I'm serious."

Beverley could see this was no laughing matter and indicated her desire to listen by slowing her level of activity and leaning in closer.

"This evening," he continued, "before Austen woke me up to ask could she go to the mall with you, I was having this dream that I was Scrooge and the ghost of Jacob Marley was that rich guy, Ernest Bell, the one who committed suicide. He showed up wearing all these chains that represented greed and he was telling me how . . . how he had spent his whole life making money and not caring about people and now he was cursed and had to walk the earth as penance."

Beverley was mesmerized less by the story than with his candor. He seemed lost in another world trying desperately to figure a way home. It was plain to see that this revelation, though a dream, had stirred something real in him.

"Here's the weird part," he continued, "after you brought Austen home, I put her to bed and after I got out the shower I imagined I saw him again, staring at me in the mirror. This time he was warning me, telling me how I was neglecting Austen's happiness and the only way I could save myself was through a visit by some spirits."

"When? Tonight?"

"Yeah. It was supposed to happen at eleven o'clock."

"Like in 'A Christmas Carol'?" she added skeptically.

"Yeah, just like in the book."

Was this his version of a Christmas ghost story with her fireplace doubling as the campfire? She searched his eyes for any sign of deception but saw nothing that would indicate he was trying to pull her leg. The fact that he was not asking her opinion in the matter told her that he was serious.

"Is that why you came over here?" she asked, trying not to make a cheap and obvious joke of his intentions.

His only response was a brief smile accompanied with a quick shake of his head. He avoided any eye contact as though embarrassed she had knowingly caught him in a lie.

It all made sense now. She thought about his inability to relax and the edginess he displayed during the wind event. *That was around eleven o'clock, wasn't it?* Whatever it was he had experienced had spooked him to the point that he needed to reveal it in order to give it substance. Whether real or imagined, it had affected him deeply, forcing him to reexamine his attitude about Christmas even though he had tried his best to relegate it to the ranks of triviality.

Finally, a crack in his well-crafted armor was showing. Beneath the previously impenetrable exterior, a sliver of vulnerability was shining. His unprovoked disclosure created a new dimension and gave her a reason to look at him in a different light. By confiding a secret and searching for an ally to share in his suspicion, he was reaching out to her. If she chose to ridicule him, he would retreat and close the door forever. If she accepted and nurtured his frail admission, maybe, just maybe, he would begin to trust her emotionally and they could start to engage each other on a more expressive level.

"Well, whatever the reason, I'm glad you came over. I'm enjoying the company."

He was expecting her to dismiss his claim and make a joke of it as she usually did, but her subtle though skillful deflection offered him the opportunity to appreciate her ability to listen and empathize without judgment.

The mood in the room had definitely changed. Both felt as though they had weathered a storm together and though headed for uncharted waters, were willing to work together to ensure smooth sailing.

He raised his head and looked at her as if seeing her for the first time and said with feeling, "So am I."

Reinvigorated like a sinner after confession, he edged closer and rubbed his hands together enthusiastically, "Hand me the next gift on the list."

"Are you sure you're ready to try another one?"

"Just give it here and watch me work, woman. I'll show you how this is done."

Beverley smiled and handed him a small box, suddenly wishing she had more gifts to wrap. Arthur did not know it, but this was turning out to be one of the best Christmas Eves she had spent in a long time.

CHAPTER 15

It was already a difficult enough job trying to keep Christmas Present focused on the mundane details of everyday life, but with the thought of visiting a human rattling around in his head, it was proving near impossible. Before she lost her mind completely to frustration, Claire decided to delay her briefing until he had settled on what to wear on his visit.

Though he wore the same thing everyday he was nonetheless a meticulous dresser who doted on every detail. Tonight's attire would be the same. He would wear a red wool-blend suit and vest with a green pocket square, a plain white shirt with 'GCP' monogrammed on each sleeve, a red and white striped tie, and two-toned patent leather shoes with red socks patterned by tiny, white, striped candy canes. The only accessories would be ruby cufflinks in the shape of snowflakes and a green Christmas tree tie tack.

On blustery days, he would sometimes wear a green, wool neck scarf and a red wool overcoat, but Claire did not know why since he was immune to the cold.

With less than an hour to go before his departure to the Fisher home, he was wasting time primping in front of a full-length mirror.

"Which one should I wear?" he asked holding out a set of identical red and white striped ties for Claire to inspect. "This one . . . or this one?"

"They're both the same, sir," she sighed.

"No, they're not," he argued. "This one is red with white stripes," he clarified pushing it closer for her to see. "And this one . . . is white with red stripes."

"Whatever," huffed Claire, checking the time. She was ahead of schedule but wanted to finish her brief so he could have enough time to go over his notes before leaving. She decided to quit wasting time arguing with him and just agree with whatever choices he made. They were all the same anyway.

"Go with that one," she said pointing without bothering to look.

"I like this one, too," he agreed and began untying the identical red and white striped tie he was already wearing.

While he was occupied, Claire seized upon the chance to continue her brief. "I've updated your hand held with all the necessary information. My cell and home phone numbers will pop up the minute you turn it on just in case you forget anything and need to call me. The GPS has both locations, there and here, pre-programmed. And, sir?"

"Yes?"

"Try not to lose it," she begged though she intended it to sound more like a warning. "The last time it took us three days to find you."

"I don't remember that."

"I do! I spent so much time here my husband thought I was having an affair!"

Satisfied with his tie, he nonetheless readjusted the knot and moved his attention to his jacket. Claire shook her head imagining what marriage to a man as obsessive as he would be like. *We would definitely have to have separate closets and bathrooms.* Now, he was trying different buttoning combinations on his jacket, turning side to side to see which profile was the most fashionable and flattering.

"What do you think, one button or two? Maybe I should just leave the jacket open." He stuck his hands in his pocket and struck a casual but reckless pose.

Claire had seen enough of his charades and continued her brief in a pitched tone meant to warn him against distracting her.

"The Ghost of Christmas Past will be finished by eleven-fifty. You arrive at midnight sharp. I recorded some talking points for you, so here," she handed him an earpiece, "wear this and follow the prompts. Start wrapping up around twelve forty-five, and leave no later than twelve-fifty. That will give him some time for reflection before the Ghost of Christmas Future arrives at one."

"The only change is," she paused long enough to thumb through a few pages of her itinerary, "instead of visiting the daughter, Austen, you'll be visiting the father, Arthur."

"Why's that? She wrote the letter."

"All kids who believe in Santa Claus have Christmas spirit. The only way it can be ruined is by an adult, and since that is her dad, he is legally responsible. His information is all here including a picture. You have about half an hour so please try to spend some time reviewing. Okay?"

"Okay."

She placed the folder containing his itinerary along with the handheld device on his desk.

"Any questions?"

"Yeah, one last thing," he said holding his finger aloft indicating he wanted her to wait for a few seconds.

He opened the closet door and nearly was lost to sight as he plunged headlong into the abyss rummaging through boxes on the floor like a child trying to locate a lost toy. Moments later, he emerged holding two pairs of shoes that he held up for Claire's inspection.

"Which do you think I should go with? Red leather lace up's, or red leather slip-on's?"

Claire exhaled a long sigh as she deflated against the door, staring at the ceiling. *Why me?*

CHAPTER 16

The image of the North Pole marketed to humans by the brand managers at Kringle & Kringle Advertising fell ridiculously short of reality. The idea of pixyish elves sitting around picnic tables in log cabin workshops hammering away at little wooden trucks was about as accurate as Keebler Elves baking cookies in hollowed out trees. Rudolph the Red Nosed Reindeer, the Grinch and Frosty the Snowman were nothing more than sophisticated ad campaigns used to manage and market the biggest brand in the world: Christmas. Because of their creative genius it was the king of all holidays, its reach so widespread it was now referred to as a 'season'. It had become an integral part of the human psyche, as natural and accepted as gravity.

As for the real denizens of the North Pole, everyday was not Christmas. They fell victim to the same stresses of life that clouded humanity's existence. Though crime was virtually nonexistent and limited to the usual shenanigans of adolescent elves (teenagers were teenagers everywhere it seemed), other social ills such as unemployment, homelessness and health care concerns were as alien to them as real humans. So shielded by ignorance of the outside world, life as it was, was relative bliss.

All, however, did not share such a simplistic view of the world. Ignorance was a trait neither embodied nor tolerated by the Ghost of Christmas Past. She championed the axiom, 'with knowledge comes understanding', and therefore, expected those possessing knowledge to understand its unlimited potential and utilize it for the improvement of themselves and others.

For centuries, she had watched as human intellect ebbed and flowed like the tides, powerful in its surge but destined to retreat over and over again. Instead of learning from their mistakes and evolving in a consistent manner, the human race had traced a haphazard route toward enlightenment. Their best intentions may have been motivated by sound ideals, but more times than not their best laid plans routinely fell short, usurped by greed and eventually defaulting to the path of least resistance. Such short sidedness embraced by a race of people with limited life spans, condemned them to a monotonous cycle of creation and erosion leaving only destruction as their ultimate legacy.

Living in the North Pole, she had languished in obscurity, servicing human needs and had grown tired of their hubris in accomplishments that meant little in the grand scheme of things. They misappropriated the talents of their best and brightest to devise new ways of destroying each other instead of advancing humanity's cause. If the only thing they respected were power and control, she would give them an exercise in the application of both.

The Ghost of Christmas Past held Austen's hand firmly, pulling her along. The click of her fashionably conscious stiletto heals echoed through the bleak corridor in a sinister military cadence. Unbeknownst to Austen, she was a victim on two fronts. Not only was she a captive of Christmas Past but also a captive of savvy marketing. She thought she knew a great deal about Santa Claus and his tiny toy-making hamlet, but nowhere in any text or pictures were there descriptions or images of dark, damp stone corridors that seemed as endless and intimidating as the one she found herself led through by Christmas Past. If anything, thought Austen, this was more like a dungeon right out the pages of 'The Count of Monte Cristo'. Where were the snowmen, reindeers, elves and toys? She wanted to ask but decided to wait, after all, they were on their way to see Santa Claus. Austen's suspicions heightened when they stopped in front of a large wooden door.

"Is this where your friend lives?"

"Yes," Christmas Past replied without bothering to look at Austen. "He's waiting for us inside."

Christmas Past released her grip, then placed her gloved hand against the door. Austen stepped back and grew wide-eyed as the knotty timbers began to groan and move, awakened by Christmas Past's touch. Slowly, yet surely, an aged face began to form, its features contorting and writhing against the grain as though pained by the effort to take shape. Once materialized, the large eyes slowly opened and cast a weary glance at Austen before fixing its gaze upon Christmas Past and gaping its wooden lips to speak.

"Once comes Christmas every year,
To those who hold it sacred near,
Three Spirits know my secrets dear,
For entry, speak them slow and clear,
Five words to grant thee entry here."

"The past is future's present," said Christmas Past impatiently.

The door's eyes glanced at Austen once more, then slowly shut. Christmas Past nudged Austen aside as the massive door groaned, then emitted a sharp crack like wood being snapped and eased open just enough for her to grab its edge and pull it open.

Christmas Past took Austen by the shoulder, ushering her inside, where the sights and sounds of a menagerie of animals in cages greeted her. The welcoming committee was led by a variety of monkeys who raced to the front of their cages and stood with arms outstretched, ready to shake hands. Their animated voices created a cacophony that reverberated throughout the lab, much to the delight of Austen.

Dominating the facing wall of the makeshift laboratory was a series of chalkboards completely covered with mathematical and scientific equations the likes of which Austen had never seen. To her right were rows of concrete slab tables filled with a complex maze of glass tubing and vials that held colorful chemicals under boil and spewing noxious fumes. Behind them were bookshelves that reached to the ceiling and held few books. Instead, glass jars containing specimens of animal and human organs encased in formaldehyde filled the shelves. It was fortunate for Austen that she was too young to grasp and understand the implications of what lie around her.

The reverie of the animal circus immediately stopped the moment Christmas Past stepped inside the lab. As she stalked by with Austen in tow, the monkeys quickly retreated into the corner of their respective cages, hid their faces and cowered with fear. The rats, mice and guinea pigs tried their best to bury themselves under the layer of sawdust coating the floor of their cages leaving the rabbits to simply sit as still as possible until the threat had passed.

Standing in the middle of the lab, Christmas Past pointed to a chair and as if speaking to a dog, commanded Austen to, "Sit."

Austen, anxious to meet Santa Claus, wondered if this was some part of his toy-making factory, asked, "When are --"

Before she could complete another syllable, Christmas Past spun and in a voice filled with so much ferocity, it made her flinch, shouted, "Sit down and be quiet! You will speak only when you are spoken to!"

Tears began to well in Austen's eyes as she hurried to the chair and sat on her hands as Christmas Past scanned the Lab.

"Dr. Hamilton! Where are you? Come forth!"

Bowed by years of fatigue and anguish at his assigned task, Dr. Hamilton's thin frame, already old when last seen on the airplane, gradually surfaced from amongst the tangled weave of science dragging a left leg with a hip cramped by arthritis. Any hope of liberation had long since vanished and left him broken, both mentally and physically.

Austen wiped her eyes and focused on the old man. This was not Santa Claus. The sight of the feeble scientist made her shrink with concern. Unable to determine why they were even here, she paid careful attention to every word in an effort to discern who he was and why Christmas Past had yelled at her.

"Yes?" he answered in a voice as haggard as he appeared.

"Time is your enemy now, Doctor," threatened Christmas Past. "Have you made the necessary adjustments?"

"Yes. It should work this time."

"Should?" Her question contained an implicit warning.

"It *will* work this time," he quickly corrected.

"Good." Pleased with his response, Christmas Past kept her eyes on the doctor and began removing her gloves with measured care, pulling each finger as though preparing to sit and enjoy a meal. Once removed, she folded them with equal care and deposited them inside her purse. "Because you will be administering this dose personally."

Dr. Hamilton turned his head slightly to verify her last statement. "Huh? Me?"

"Yes. If it doesn't work this time, blood will be on your hands."

"No, I – I can't," he stuttered.

"Oh? Why is that, Doctor?" She kept her eyes steady on him as she stepped closer. "Is it because you have been purposely sabotaging your efforts in order to foil my plans? Hmmm?"

Trapped in a web of attempted deceit, Dr. Hamilton submissively dipped his head and searched the floor for any remnants of mercy.

Christmas Past closed the distance between them slowly and spoke in a measured tone that hovered somewhere between calm and calamity.

"Might I remind you, Doctor, I have spent the better part of a century meticulously drawing up and reviewing every detail of an elaborate blueprint, the cornerstone of which required a man of your talents. In a relative matter of moments, the capstone of those efforts will be placed and seal the fate of many, including your own. My patience, though considerably longer than your lifetime, has ended."

Christmas Past placed a finger under his chin, lifting his face to meet hers.

"Those who choose to forget their past," she quietly informed him, "sometimes need to relive it."

Staring into his frightened eyes, she extended her forefinger and touched his forehead. He immediately grew lightheaded as an aura of remembrance enveloped his senses. The lab faded into darkness and he saw himself falling, coiling through time and space; a vortex of images from his past, present and potential futures spun around him in no particular order, transporting him back to a fateful day of his distant youth.

IT WAS HIS DESIRE TO PROVE TO THE OLDER BOYS in the neighborhood that he was every bit their equal that caused 8-year-old Charles Hamilton to climb out of bed at one o'clock in the morning when everyone else was sleeping and search under his bed for the cigarette stolen earlier from the pack in his father's jacket pocket.

Finding the stick of tobacco, he tiptoed to the door and pressed his ear against it, then cracked it open and listened for any sound coming from his parents' bedroom just down the hallway. Hearing only the intermittent snore of his father, he locked the door, sat on his bed and lit the cigarette with a kitchen match.

The initial scent of the burning tobacco was sweet, fooling him into believing its source flavorful and mild. Like his mentors, the willing protégé sucked in a chest full of the hot air, tried to hold it, then exhale it through his nose like the snort of a mad bull.

His tender lungs were no match for the harshness of the unfiltered plant. He felt his throat constrict and a second later he was on his knees doubled over in the throes of a hacking cough.

The stream of light from the hallway sneaked under the door and alerted him a concerned mother was on her way to check on her child. She would throw open the door in a matter of seconds and if she smelled smoke, would wake his father, guaranteeing a whipping on the spot.

In a preemptive move, he staggered to his feet, stepped into the hallway, careful to close the door behind him, and met his mother half way. He assured her he was fine and on his way downstairs to get a glass of water to quell the tickling in his throat that was causing the cough.

She warned him not to drink too much before returning to her room.

The cool water soothed his parched throat, and he smiled at how easy he had deceived his mother. He reminded himself the next time he smoked, he would have to take smaller puffs and looked forward to learning how to blow smoke rings like his grandfather.

Returning to his bedroom, he never smelled the smoke on the other side of the door. The first indication came when he burned his hand on the doorknob heated by the fire within. In his panic to deny his mother entry, he had flicked the lit cigarette under his bed, but it had landed in the fold of a bed sheet. In the time it had taken him to sell his mother the well-crafted lie, the cotton sheet was ablaze and igniting the mattress while he was drinking water downstairs. Starved of air, it smoldered, waiting for him to open the door and give it the needed fuel to transform embers into a roaring inferno.

Rushed from the house, he looked over his father's shoulder and could see the flames racing throughout the upstairs, sending billowing clouds of dark smoke through windows shattered from the heat. His father set him on the curb and yelled to the growing crowd of curious neighbors to call the fire department.

He started crying at the sight of his mother crying, her head buried in his father's chest. At their feet, his little sister sat playing with her doll. The five-year-old was too young to comprehend the scope of the tragedy unfolding in front of her. Perhaps that was the reason she ran back into the house to find her missing cat, Lila. His father did not see her enter, but his mother did and ran after the child screaming. His father issued orders for Charles to stay where he was and ran into the burning house after his wife and daughter.

They never came out.

SUCH WAS THE MEMORY THAT NOW HELD Dr. Hamilton tightly within its terrifying grasp.

"No! Stop it! No!" he cried. The weight of his remembrance was so great it painfully dropped him to his knees and racked his body with grief.

"As you see, Doctor," Christmas Past warned with the point of a well-manicured finger, "She who controls your past also controls your present, and any future you may be lucky enough to see."

The sound of his sobs filled the lab and sent a shudder through Austen and the caged animals. Both are born with two traits intact, curiosity and the ability to hide when they sense fear. Austen had heard and seen enough. Sensing that whatever fate had befallen Dr. Hamilton by the hand of Christmas Past was probably meant for her as well, Austen knew she had to run away as far and fast as she could. She took a sidelong glance at the door and saw it remained slightly ajar. It looked heavy, but she was sure she could ease it open wide enough for her to slip through while Christmas Past's back was turned.

She eased from her chair and carefully edged backwards toward the door keeping her eyes fixed on Christmas Past. Once there, she leaned against it, slowly forcing it open enough to squeeze through. Once outside, she eased the door back to its original position to cover her escape.

Liberated from the threat within, all she had to do was find a place to hide until her father could come and get her.

She turned and froze in her tracks. Hovering silently in front of and peering down at her was none other than the Ghost of Christmas Future.

CHAPTER 17

Capacity crowds of revelers filled Santa Square. Thousands had gathered for the annual 'Countdown to Christmas Celebration', awaiting the highly anticipated liftoff of Santa's sleigh.

Just above the heads of the screaming crowd stood platforms manned by commentators covering the event. The largest booth belonged to NPTV Channel 12. They were the North Pole's most popular station and news leader. None other than the perennially handsome, flaxen haired anchorman, Cole Winter, and his well-endowed blond bimbo sidekick, Holly Bush, hosted the night's event.

The crowd, many of whom had been drinking since arrival earlier in the day, roared with drunken glee at every comment.

"The anticipation is building here at Santa Square!" Cole exaggerated in his best anchorman voice. "In less than twenty minutes Santa's sleigh will lift off and send this crowd into a frenzy!"

As if cued on command (they were for television ratings sake), the crowd roared and began chanting like drunks at a frat house party, "Fren-Z, fren-Z, fren-Z . . ."

Anxious to upstage her co-host and give her breasts more air time, Holly turned to the camera and reported in her best head cheerleader voice, "We're waiting for the hangar doors to open, and I can tell you, Cole, that when they do, this crowd is going to explode!"

"X-plode, X-plode, X-plode!" chanted the local chapter.

~ Click ~.

"Ugh!" exclaimed Claire switching off the television. "Those perky clowns get on my nerves." She packed up her belongings in preparation to leave for the night. Santa always scheduled a press conference before departing and all department heads were required to attend. Since Christmas Present was going on a visit, she was standing in for him and did not want to be late.

She popped her head inside his office to say goodbye, but really wanted to make sure he was studying his notes and answer any last minute questions he may have had.

"Sir, I'm heading over to the press conference. You have any questions."

"Ahhh, no. I think I have a handle on everything." He did not sound all that sure of himself, nonetheless, she knew from experience he would be fine. Once he arrived at his destination, his natural charm and cheerful spirit would win over Mr. Fisher and put him at ease. After that, Christmas Present would show him all the things he was missing in his life and set him on a course destined for charity and good will.

It would be a wonderful respite from Christmas Past's visit. She tended to be a little heavy handed in her selection of human memories to exploit. Reliving painful moments when they were clearly not at their best usually left humans more depressed than hopeful. Claire suspected she did this as a joke. It was her way of making Christmas Present's visit more difficult and giving him a hard time since she considered him 'Santa's pet'.

"Have a safe trip and call me if you need anything, okay?"

"Okay. Thanks."

"You're welcome. And don't worry, sir, you'll be fine." She waved goodbye then added, "Oh, don't forget to call me as soon as you get back. I want to hear how everything went."

"I will. Have a good time."

He crept behind and spied from the edge of his office's outer door as she walked down the corridor and entered the elevator. Satisfied she was gone, he hurried back to his office, positioned himself in front of the full-length mirror and picked up where he left off just before she entered.

"Yo, what up? I'm the Ghost of Christmas Present . . . and you are?" *Nah, a little too informal.*

"Hello, I am the Ghost of Christmas Present." *Better, but not so official. You're there to help him, not scare him.*

"Hello, Mr. Fisher. How are you tonight, sir? I am the one and only Ghost of the present Christmas season." *Not bad, a little wordy. Clean it up and I think we have it.*

"Good morning, Mr. Fisher. I am the Ghost of Christmas Present. It's a pleasure to meet you, sir." *Oh yeah, that's the one!*

While Christmas Present was busy rehearsing his entry, Austen cowered waiting for the reprimand that was surely coming, but the Ghost of Christmas Future said nothing. She tried to look at its face to determine whether this was a friend or foe, but the large hood of the floor length cowl confined the face to shadow. Curiosity got the better of her. She stretched out her arm, parted the seam of the cloak and peered into darkness.

Removing her hand, she breathed a sigh of relief. Perhaps it was just an empty cloak left hanging there for Christmas Past. She looked up and down the dark corridor trying to decide which way to run when the arm of the cloak slowly rose and reached for her. She shrieked, pulled the door open and ran inside towards the sympathetic face of Dr. Hamilton with the Ghost of Christmas Future drifting in behind her. Before she could reach her destination, Christmas Past grabbed her arm and pulled her near.

"I though I told you not to move!" she scolded. She dragged Austen toward her assigned chair and roughly thrust her onto it. "Now sit there and do not move, or else!" she threatened.

The Ghost of Christmas Future hovered behind Austen blocking any thought or path of future escape, leaving Christmas Past to refocus her attention on Dr. Hamilton.

"Now Doctor, do I have your assurance that you have perfected the solution?"

Still reeling from his episode, he simply nodded 'yes'.

"Well then . . . prepare it."

UNDERSTANDABLY, DR. HAMILTON REFUSED TO touch another cigarette after that fateful day and grew to despise the habit of smoking. By the time he had entered medical school, he was keenly aware of the growing grip of nicotine addiction on society. After reading about similar tragedies caused by smokers who had fallen asleep with lit cigarettes dangling from their lips and fingers, he decided to focus his studies on the long term health affects to discredit the industry's aggressive propaganda hidden under the auspices of advertising.

By the mid 1960's, he had become a researcher and had joined a handful of scientists on the cusp of understanding the physiological effects of nicotine on brain chemistry. He expanded his research into the affects of a wide variety of stimuli on brain chemistry and its associated behavioral effects. This had led to groundbreaking work on nasal treatments that would not only break the cycle of a variety of addictions, but also created the prospect of developing effective ways to modify abnormal behavior.

Published extensively throughout the world, other researchers had read his scientific papers and began building upon his theories. Now in the twilight of his years, the nomination for the Nobel Prize in Medicine was his reward for his genius.

Unfortunately, it was the also the reason Christmas Past had drafted him, so to speak, to head a certain research project of her own.

AS DR. HAMILTON APPROACHED WITH A SMALL VIAL of liquid attached to an atomizer, Christmas Future moved aside letting Christmas Past take up residence behind Austen. She placed her hands on her shoulders, pinning Austen in place, and then directed her attention toward Dr. Hamilton.

"Administer it," Christmas Past ordered.

"To her?" the Doctor questioned hesitantly.

The look of impatience infused with the promise of violence on Christmas Past's face answered his ridiculous question. His hands shook as he bent to position the atomizer closer to Austen's nostrils, and then wilted as he stared into her timid eyes.

A variety of factors - age, stress, even the residual effects of his journey through time, could have easily accounted for what happened next. Whatever it was, as Austen squirmed under the clutch of Christmas Past, he looked into her eyes and saw the terrified face of his little sister as she called out for her father to save her on that fateful night.

"Daddy! Help me! Daddy!" She screamed as the flames licked at her feet.

Dr. Hamilton recoiled in fear at the sound of Austen's voice. "Let me go! I want my daddy. I want my daddy! Let me go!"

"I can't do it. I won't!" he pleaded staggering backwards. "She's a child for God's sake! A child!"

Christmas Past released her grip on Austen and angrily stalked Dr. Hamilton. "Give me the vial," she demanded.

Summoning what little courage he had left, he hobbled away as he openly challenged her authority.

"No! I won't let you do it . . . not to an innocent child! No!"

"Give me that vial," shouted Christmas Past. "NOW!"

Dr. Hamilton turned and limped toward the corner of the lab as Christmas Past raced to intercept his clumsy retreat. He pulled the atomizer from the vial and held the precious liquid over a vat of acid.

"NO! Let her go or I swear I'll destroy it!" His face filled with rage as he leveled his eyes at Christmas Past, his voice resounding with contempt and moral outrage.

"It will take weeks to distill another batch! I don't care what you do to me! I won't let you use this on a child!"

Christmas Past stopped in her tracks and searched his face for any sign that he was bluffing, but found none. She had miscalculated his resolve and silently applauded his deft move while cursing herself for not anticipating this latest hitch. She glanced at her watch. It was 11:35. Time was *her* enemy now. Santa's press conference was moments away and after that he would be leaving to make his deliveries. She needed proof the formula worked before his sleigh departed.

As she glared at Dr. Hamilton, her mind was filtering a series of scenarios in rapid succession. She could test his resolve. After all, he was an old man incapable of reacting to any sudden moves. She calculated the time it would take her to close the distance and seize the vial before he emptied it into the acid. That was a possibility, but if he suddenly dropped the vial instead of trying to empty the contents, it would be lost.

Physically turning back the hands of time was not an option in the North Pole. Too many residents were spirits or sprites, immune to the effect; besides, Santa would feel the spatial disturbance and make inquiries.

There was also the possibility that the formula he now held was still incomplete. She could not be sure. Such scheming on his part was unlikely, but possible. He had fooled her twice already so there was no need to doubt his manipulation. She could not take the chance.

The thought of a human duping her infuriated her, forcing

her to take a step towards the frightened doctor. No sooner had she edged forward, he held his breath and tilted the bottle, releasing a few precious drops into the vat of acid which sizzled and bubbled at the opportunity to prove it could completely destroy anything, given a chance.

His resolve proven, she conceded. "Alright, Doctor. Congratulations, you win," She backed away and pulled Austen to her feet.

"I will take her home and return shortly with a more suitable subject to whom you will, and I do mean *will*, administer the formula. Make certain it is ready or I can assure you certain elements of your past will make for a rather unpleasant future."

The Ghost of Christmas Future hovered in the dark passageway as Christmas Past shoved Austen inside the storeroom where she first encountered the deceitful Spirit.

"There is no escape from this room. Quietly remain here until I return to take you home." Christmas Past straightened and expelled a snort of regret at the day's misfortunes. Before exiting, she looked back at Austen seated on one of the many boxes stacked high in the room. "Don't worry, you're just having a bad dream. In the morning, you will wake up to a glorious Christmas morning and won't remember a thing." She pulled the door shut and locked it.

In the stony corridor, Christmas Past checked her watch and beckoned Christmas Future closer with a wave of her hand. "Find her father, Arthur, and bring him here before Christmas Present makes his arrival. I'll keep her here as insurance to make sure the doctor cooperates."

Christmas Future nodded once in approval and immediately faded from view, leaving Christmas Past to clench her fists in rage.

It had never been her intention for Christmas Future to bring Austen to the North Pole. It was her father, Arthur, she wanted. After the earlier failed trial on Ernest Bell and the more recent Salvation Army Volunteer, Christmas Past needed to identify another subject. When she received the knowledge of Christmas Present's visit to the Fisher house, it all fell into place.

Normally, she was the first ghost to show up at eleven, but she needed the time to look back and 'review' the past and investigate her suspicions about Dr. Hamilton's suspected sabotage of the formula. With time running short, she decided to send Christmas Future in her place. Unlike the past, the future was fluid, changing constantly depending on a person's actions in the present. It had been her responsibility to visit Arthur first, set the table for Christmas Present who in turn prepared the way for Christmas Future. With the order of appearance disrupted, Christmas Future had no way of knowing the plan to visit Austen had changed to Arthur, which was the reason Christmas Future had brought Austen instead. It had been a costly error on her part.

Christmas Past's strength lay in her ability to chart the rise and fall of human action and emotion, and then extrapolate motivations from the past and apply them to the present and sometimes, the future. This ability allowed her the luxury of being able to 'predict' what they would do at any given moment with deadly accuracy. Errors were inevitable; yet the cycle of behavior that humans were prone to following overrode the minute glitches and ultimately averaged out in her favor.

Historically, humans were creatures of habit. They shopped at the same stores, ate the same types of meals, watched the same types of television shows, etc. The more they aged, the more certain their routines, making it easier to predict their tendencies. Arthur was a single father and always remained at home on Christmas Eve. There was no need to assume he would alter that schedule, therefore, she could not have anticipated his departure from the premises, leaving Austen alone. With time running out, she had had little choice but to use the child as her guinea pig.

The same reasoning had applied to Dr. Hamilton. Nothing in his past that indicated he was capable of mounting such deception or opposition. His placid demeanor along with his genius was the reason Christmas Past had chosen him to lead her research.

She snorted with disgust at the momentary setback then calmed herself. *There was still ample time.* Arthur would be there shortly, after which she would proceed with her plan and complete past business.

CHAPTER 18

Beverley decided to take a break and join Arthur on the floor watching the fire and listening to music. She had wrapped all of the gifts needed to hand out to friends and their children on her visits tomorrow afternoon. The others could wait until tomorrow night. Some she would put in the mail, the remainder she would take with her when she drove south to bring in the New Year with her family.

She had planned to stay up half the night wrapping gifts, but Arthur's presence was unexpected and now, most welcome. After his recent admission about seeing a ghost, the friendly though acerbic sparring that comprised the backbone of their tenuous friendship over the years, now seemed silly and wasted.

Before joining Arthur, she had changed her Christmas play list of upbeat sing-alongs like 'Santa Claus is Coming to Town', 'Jingle Bell Rock' and 'Deck the Halls' to a slower, more contemplative selection that included, 'What Child is This?,' 'O Little Town of Bethlehem' and a few instrumentals.

The softer soundtrack matched the glow of the fireplace they shared and made it easier for her to ask a question that had been on her mind since her first Christmas as his neighbor.

"What do you have against celebrating Christmas?"

"Which one?" he chuckled. "Jesus' birthday, Santa's deadline, or the end of the corporate pick pocketing season."

"Geez, you are such a cynic!" she decried, elbowing him in the ribs. "I know its gotten out of hand, I agree with you a hundred percent, but Austen doesn't understand all that. All she knows is her friends believe in Santa Claus and have Christmas trees and she doesn't."

She was expecting Arthur to respond but when he did not, she realized he agreed with her. His eyes, unblinking and focused on the dancing flames told her there was more to this. His reserve emanated from an emotional source and if she wanted to reach him her appeal would have to reach deeper into his psyche.

"Childhood should be the best years of your life. Christmas, Thanksgiving and birthdays . . . those are the highlights. They're the memories you carry with you forever. Parents should do everything to make sure they're happy ones."

"You're right," he said softly, as if responding to a voice deep within.

Feeling as though she had finally reached him, she pleaded her case. "So what's wrong with letting her believe in Santa Claus? She is going to find out soon enough he isn't real, why do you have to tell her? What's the harm?"

Arthur continued to stare into the fire as if he were waiting for it to whisper the answer. Not wanting him to feel she was being confrontational in any way, she followed his gaze and immediately regretted pressing him. She leaned her head on his shoulder and placed her hand on his wrist, squeezing it softly, offering her touch as an apology for trespassing into territory she had no business entering.

His response, though barely audible, resounded loud and clear.

"I don't like lying to her."

Austen pinched herself. *Ouch.* She remembered hearing that if you pinched yourself and felt it, it meant you were awake. The touch of reality made her painfully aware of her dire situation. This was no dream. She was not at the North Pole, and she was not going to meet Santa Claus. The mean lady calling herself the Ghost of Christmas Past had lied to her. Kidnapped for whatever reason, if she was going to escape or help her father and the police find her, she would first have to figure out where she was.

On television and in the movies, the police often listened to background noises to help them pinpoint locations of hostages. She did not remember being driven anywhere, nor had she walked outside which meant that Christmas Past must have carried her here. For all she knew, she was relatively close to home and tried to remember where some large businesses were located.

Since her arrival, she had been keenly aware of the muffled din of a factory or some kind of plant nearby, but in her excitement, then fear, had paid it no attention. Now held against her will, it provided the only real hope of escape.

The only place that came to mind was the Ports Authority on the waterfront where large container ships from all over the world deposited their cargo. It was a few miles from their home and she could hear the constant loading and unloading of trailers by the large cranes from the house. For all she knew, she was sitting in one of the large warehouses surrounding the port.

When seeking solutions to complicated problems, it was always best to start with the easiest. She tiptoed toward the door and pressed her ear against it. Hearing nothing, she pulled on the handle, and then remembered hearing Christmas Past lock it from the outside. With her back against the door, she took a thorough scan of her surroundings. It was the standard large storeroom filled with boxes.

She tilted her glance upward and saw three small openings where light filtered through. Somewhere beyond the vents was where the sounds of production were coming from. If she could somehow climb up there, she could look out and maybe see a landmark telling her exactly where she was.

She pushed one of the boxes to see how heavy it was. Though cumbersome due to their size (some were nearly half her size), she was able to push them with little effort. Maneuvering them to create crude steps, she carefully climbed higher, pushing and pulling them into position until she was within arms reach of the overhead vent.

Perched precariously at the top, she grabbed hold of the grate and pulled herself to a standing position. The vent gave a floor level view of the main gift-wrapping facility. She pressed her face close against the vent in an effort to increase her peripheral view. From her vantage point, she could see cardboard boxes of all sizes being carried along a conveyor and disappearing around the corner.

Suddenly out of nowhere, she heard the sound of wheels and someone singing a Christmas song. Her eyes grew wide at the sight of an elf pushing a handcart and wearing headphones. She was sure he was an elf. Though he was not wearing the traditional green garb and peppermint stripped stockings like the elves she had seen in book illustrations, his somewhat diminutive size and pointed ears told her that this was indeed an elf.

The revelation shocked her. *Santa's elves! I am at the North Pole!* He was standing less than thirty feet away from her. She yelled as loud as she could but the mechanized din of the facility drowned out her tiny voice. If he only took off his earphones for a second, he possibly would have heard her frantic cry.

She watched in desperation as he loaded a box onto the conveyor and then danced off in the opposite direction with his hand truck in tow.

Annoyed by her failure, she slapped her hand against the grate. Her act of frustration proved unwise. Perched high on an unsteady stairwell of boxes, her sudden movement caused it to sway. She maneuvered her body, trying to steady the shifting column, but that only increased its instability and soon she was tumbling headlong down a ramp of cardboard.

It was lucky for her that science and nature made allowances for babies and children falling. Adults usually tensed during falls and increased their chances of injury. She landed on the top of a cardboard box that gave way under her weight and came to rest on her back.

Her fall had broken the box's seal and agitated the contents. As she struggled to free herself, contorting as an angry cat held too long, a muffled voice emanated from within.

"Hello, my name is Cleosistah."

Austen froze and listened. Was the Ghost of Christmas Past playing another trick on her? After witnessing her power, she could take nothing for granted. A few moments passed before she tried to regain her feet. Once again, the muffled voice spoke.

"What's your name?"

This time she clearly heard the voice. Realizing it was coming from inside the box beneath her, she peeled away the packing tape, and then gently lifted the flaps. Facing her was the smiling face of a life-sized doll folded at the waist. She rushed to remove the packing material and in pulling the doll from its carrier, activated the voice once again.

"Do you want to be my friend? I want to be yours."

Austen propped the doll against the box and stared at it. It was a modern day African-American version of its ancient namesake, Cleopatra. A metal band around her head held her shoulder length twisted braids in place. Her eyes, wide and colorfully painted, were facsimiles of the Pharaoh's hieroglyphic portrait. Austen reached out and pushed Cleosistah's chest.

"Do you want to go outside and play?" she asked.

"No, I want my daddy. I want to go home," replied Austen.

Feeling scared and alone, Austen sat and hugged the doll close.

"Can we go outside and play?" it asked sweetly.

"No," answered Austen, and started to cry.

CHAPTER 19

Santa Claus and his wife held hands as they stood on the red carpet. Reporters from the various North Pole publications jockeyed for position as photographers snapped photos of the pair. Shantese Kringle, Santa's wife of eight years, looked stunning as ever. Wearing a red designer dress and a white fur coat, she looked every part the trophy wife of the man who had championed the Christmas cause and beamed a knowing smile.

Santa, yielding to requests from the photographers, released his hold on his beautiful wife and let her take the spotlight as the lines of elfin Paparazzi snapped every angle as she posed for their cameras.

She had not always been this popular.

The original Mrs. Claus, known for her charitable work throughout the North Pole, had endeared herself to the community. After 120 years of marriage, they had built an alliance that stood as a testament to love and companionship and was the envy of all. It seemed unlikely that the dynamic duo would ever divorce, but after their kids were grown the seams began to show and eventually wore thin enough to sever the once harmonious partnership. Santa Claus never saw it coming and took full responsibility for their break-up.

The story was a familiar one.

Christopher Kringle was a young ambitious inventor working in his father's tiny toy factory. When his father retired, leaving him to continue the family tradition, he finally had the opportunity to execute an idea that he believed would transform the world. A full century and a half before Henry Ford would discover the merits of assembly line production and change the face of manufacturing forever; he had already worked out the details and put his vision in motion.

Within a decade, 'Kringle & Son' had transformed the North Pole. Seeking to expand the family business, the next obvious step was to start exporting to a world that seemed to need what they had to market, a unique and fun way to celebrate Christmas. After consulting with his wife, he made the unprecedented decision to travel abroad and see how other cultures celebrated the season. He enlisted the aid of the Ghost of Christmas Past, Present and Future, and together they went on a fact-finding mission to see how best to spread their message of cheer and joy. With a few well placed articles and a secretive collaboration with the well known author, Charles Dickens, to write 'A Christmas Carol', the modern framework for Christmas and how to celebrate it was well on its way to becoming a thing of legend.

From then on, Santa spent every waking moment designing, molding and refining the holiday. Driven by his fear of failure, he barely saw his children, leaving his wife to raise them while he built the business into what it had become, Christmas Industries. By the time he was satisfied he could take some time off to spend with his family, it was too late.

It was an irony not lost on him. Driven to perfect a holiday meant to bring people and families together, the joy he brought to the world had been lost on his family at home. Some would say that it was a small price to pay, but the cost to his conscience was immeasurable. The time spent away from his children haunted him and was the reason he redoubled his efforts to make sure every child would have something to smile about on Christmas day.

The announcement of the divorce of the reigning king and queen stunned the capital. The perennial couple had become the face of Christmas. Both he and his wife realized the growing importance of the season and their role in promoting its 'family' aspect with an emphasis on the children. With that in mind, they maintained an air of civility, agreed to terms on their own and separated amicably. Over the years, they continued to enjoy a close relationship. She had remarried and they lived within walking distance of each other's hamlet.

Their divorce, though accepted by residents, posed a potential image problem with marketers. How do you promote a family holiday with Santa and Mrs. Claus divorced? You don't. Rather than endorse any upheaval, for marketing purposes (to humans only), she would remain the iconic image of Mrs. Claus.

Santa checked his watch, gave a delicate wave, regained possession of his wife, and made his way towards the press conference where department heads, advisors and press awaited his arrival.

A band of elves playing the unofficial North Pole Christmas theme 'Jingle Bells' announced his entrance. The press corps stood and clapped in unison with the music as he mounted the dais and took the time to shake hands and exchanged brief thoughts with each department head representing their employees.

No one had ever mustered the courage to accuse the Ghost of Christmas Past of looking nervous, but to Santa's trained eye, the stiffness in her already rigid stance leaked a touch of anxiety.

"I'm surprised to see you back so soon. How was your visit with Mr. Fisher?" he asked with a squeeze of her fleshy shoulder.

"Excellent sir, smooth sailing as usual," she lied yet managed to stretch a terse smile across her ruby red lips.

Santa nodded approval and continued meeting and greeting his honored guests. Claire was giddy with excitement as she watched him move down the line toward her. Aware of the cameras, she tried not to openly stare. Though she worked in the same building and had occasion to see him on a regular basis, she rarely had the chance to engage him on any personal level. Given this rare opportunity, she struggled to contain her excitement.

"Claire! Good to see you here," Santa embellished.

She knew he knew her name but was stunned nonetheless to hear him say it. She felt like an insider when he leaned in close and whispered, "I know you have a difficult job, and I just want you to know how much I appreciate your patience. You've been nothing short of extraordinary."

She had rehearsed a greeting but his glowing review caught her off guard and left her speechless. She felt like Christmas Present and wished she had written her response on a note card.

"Is Christmas Present ready for his little trip?'

"Ugh, yes sir. He'll do fine," she stammered.

"He always does," he said. He patted her hand and continued down the line leaving her to judge her performance.

Finished with his personal greeting, Santa finally took his place behind the podium to applause and flashbulbs. Claire was standing in close proximity and composed herself just in case her face made it into a photographer's frame. The last thing she wanted was friends and family seeing her on the front page of the newspaper with her eyes closed and not smiling.

Santa raised his hands to quiet the crowd and patiently waited as everyone found their seats. Just as he was about to begin, Sebastian the mechanic quietly entered, eased his way onto the platform trying not to draw attention to himself and took his place next to the Ghost of Christmas Past.

As always, every station throughout the North Pole broadcast the press conference. Those not watching from the comfort of their home caught the telecast in bars and outdoor screens set up in public places for those enjoying the festivities. Even the overly raucous crowd gathered in Holly Berry Square quieted to hear Santa's words.

"I would like to thank the wonderful staff, represented here by the various department heads, for another outstanding job well done. Their commitment to maintaining the high standards of service to a grateful world is why the Christmas tradition continues to captivate and excite children of all ages."

His opening statement elicited kind applause from the guests on the platform and audience members, but outside the revelers threw up a round of cheers, whistles and yelping loud enough to raise the dead.

The light applause provided the cover Sebastian needed. Like a pickpocket passing off a mark's wallet to his partner, he deftly transferred a small keychain connected to a remote control into the Ghost of Christmas Past's hand.

"Our efforts continue to succeed because of the love and support we receive from you, the community of elves, fairies, pixies, spirits and sprites, who work tirelessly throughout the year to make this night a special one."

"But I can assure you in the coming year, our focus will remain true, our resolve strengthened, and the collective desire to share our cherished family values will continue to expand until 'peace on earth, good will towards men', is no longer a seasonal catchphrase, but a year round reality."

The short speech, though politically correct and necessary for the occasion, was mostly derivative of years before, and nonetheless brought everyone to his or her feet. He took a few questions from reporters, most of which were focused on details of the new sleigh. He deftly avoided their questions and noting the time, excused himself. The thunderous applause mixed with chants of 'Noel' as Santa waved and made his way off the stage toward his dressing room where he would be fitted into his ceremonial Santa suit. The sea of photographers raced to position themselves for the first shots when he reemerged in his official duds.

Sebastian and the Ghost of Christmas Past watched from the safety of the stage as the throng followed their leader. Her smile slowly morphed into a derisive sneer as her focus turned to the small remote control cupped in her hand. She stared at the device, lightly moving her thumb across the surface of the button, savoring the moment like hard candy on her tongue as Sebastian's face danced with anticipation. The crowd waning, she flashed Sebastian a sinister smile and depressed the button.

Deep within the undercarriage of the sleigh, past the venous network of wiring and clusters of circuitry, a nondescript black box sat securely fastened to the sleigh's frame. The only feature defining its function was a flashing green light. Moments later, it switched from flashing green to solid red.

CHAPTER 20

One of the unfortunate truths one learns later in life is that Christmas best served children and lovers. Unlike any other holiday, its power lay in the ability to wipe away a years worth of hardship and sow the seeds of renewal for the one to come.

The glow of the dying fire cast warm shadows across the faces of Beverley and Arthur, holding them in its hypnotic stare. Each silently wished the moment would last forever. Beverley had not felt this relaxed on a Christmas Eve since she was a child. As for Arthur, his last memory of a moment like this was the first Christmas he spent with his new bride, a year before Austen was born.

Beverley found herself wondering how the night would end, while Arthur contemplated what tomorrow would bring. They had clearly crossed a hurdle in a relationship that until that point had depended solely on Austen. She was the sun around which they orbited, perfectly circling on different paths, occasionally closing the distance between each other yet destined to keep moving on cautiously measured, mutually agreed upon paths. Like astronomers gazing at distant worlds through a limited lens, each admired the other from afar, mentally recorded the comings and goings, marked time by their presence and wondered what life would be like had they the ability and time to reach the other world.

It was a fatal combination of fantasy and fear. The attraction was unmistakable. As for Austen, there was no question. Whenever she and Arthur were going anywhere and happened to catch Beverley outside, the little matchmaker would make it a point to invite Beverley to go along. Her impromptu invitations left Beverley and Arthur with embarrassed smiles and errant excuses.

To avoid similar occurrences, Beverley invented an arsenal of plausible refusals to stave off participating in their family outings. As Austen grew older, Beverley grew tired of blatantly lying to the child and often beat her to the punch by creating alibis for made up activities or events she was already engaged in before Austen had the chance to even ask.

Her lies caught up with her one Saturday afternoon when she mistook Austen's intentions and announced she had some shopping to do. When Austen asked if she could go, Arthur laughed so hard at the backfire that Beverley was stuck and ended up in the mall buying yet another pair of black shoes to cover her blunder.

The largest of the logs, precariously placed on the grate, had burned unevenly and suddenly fell with a crunch sending embers scattering through the protective screen. Beverley instinctively flinched, curling her bare feet inward causing them to casually brush against Arthur's bare ankle. For the second time that night, both felt awkward and exchanged silly smiles like teenagers on a first date.

Beverley reached for the fireplace poker but Arthur quickly sat up and took the tool from her.

"Let me get that," he offered. It was the least he could do to repay her for her hospitality.

"Want me to put another log on the fire?"

"Sure, why not," granted Beverley after glancing at the time and seeing midnight rapidly approaching. With Arthur's back turned, she reached for a gift and tucked it under the quilted throw crumpled next to her. Arthur crawled back to his spot on the pillows, satisfied with his small contribution to the ambience as the flames embraced the fresh fuel. Before he had a chance to relax, she handed him the gift.

"Here. That's for you."

"You bought me a gift." Arthur remarked with genuine surprise.

"Last Christmas when I brought over Austen's gift, you looked like you were going to cry because I didn't get you anything," teased Beverley.

"I did not."

"Yes you did, and you know it."

"All right . . . maybe," he conceded lightheartedly. "But nothing came out."

He took the gift, shook it like a little kid and in his best imitation of Austen replied, "Thank you, Ms. Beverley."

She punched him playfully, and they shared a laugh that led to a spontaneous kiss on the cheek.

"You're welcome," she replied.

"I'll put it under my tree and open it first thing in the morning."

"You don't have one," she said rolling her eyes. "Go ahead, you can open it."

"But it's not Christmas, yet," he said after glancing at his watch.

"Well, when I was a kid, my parents used to let us open up one gift on Christmas Eve."

"Really?"

"My dad wouldn't let us open our presents on Christmas morning until the whole family had breakfast together. It used to make me so mad. By the time we opened our gifts and ran outside with our toys, kids in the neighborhood were already tired of playing with theirs."

Arthur rolled the present around in his hands studying how perfect the wrapping was. In the dim light, he could barely see the strategically placed transparent tape. He picked at the edges trying not to rip the paper, but failed in his first attempt and apologized with his eyes to Beverley for disfiguring her effort.

Beverley fidgeted impatiently. She seemed more anxious than he was.

"I guess I better rip it open, huh?"

"If you cared, you would."

Like a madman, he ripped into the box, shredding the wrapping to Beverley's delight until he held a plain white box. Her eyes widened as he carefully lift the lid and laughed at the sight of the gift enclosed.

"A leather bound, 'Charles Dickens Christmas'. Thank you! I watch 'A Christmas Carol' every year, but I've never read the book."

Beverley could barely contain her joy. There was nothing more exciting for a gift giver than seeing their gift strike a chord of happiness in the receiver. It was music to her ears and her entire body shook with glee. She edged closer and leaned against his shoulder to share the contents.

"It has all of Charles Dickens Christmas stories along with the original drawings," she pointed out as he thumbed through the pages looking at the finely etched illustrations. He stopped on the illustration of the Ghost of Christmas Past visiting Ebenezer Scrooge and felt a chill run through his veins at the sight of Scrooge's fearful face.

"Thank you. I really appreciate this and promise you not only will I read it, I'll read it to Austen too. Speaking of which, I need to go and check on her."

He hurried to his feet. "Hold that pose," he said placing a hand on Beverley's shoulder. "I'll be back in a minute."

"Bring back more eggnog if you have any."

"Okay."

They exchanged smiles and as he put on his jacket in the foyer. Beverley kept watch as he closed the door and tried to push back any thoughts bubbling up in her head by telling herself that this was only one night. Nonetheless, were it a date, she had seen enough to definitely ask for another.

She turned and stared into the fire, then glanced at the clock. It was 11:48. In twelve minutes, she would be bringing in Christmas with the last person she could possibly imagine sharing the moment with and could not wait until he returned.

CHAPTER 21

Steven, the Gift Coordinator, stole a concerned look at one of the many digital clocks hanging throughout the facility. It read 11:49:13. In over fifty Christmases he had never been late loading a sleigh and this year would be no exception.

"All right you slackers, start wrapping this up! We got a sleigh to finish loading! Let's go, let's go, let's go, we got orders to fill!" he pressured.

The gaggle of Inventory Control Specialists heeded his call and huddled around to receive their orders before taking off in various directions. The only specialist unaware of his command was Orlando. Dancing in space while listening to a blaring rap cover of 'Jingle Bells' from an arm-mounted iPod, the tattooed, dreadlocked elf looked as though he were the official North Pole representative for Generation 'Y'. Stephen handed him the remaining two orders, then watched with an undecided eye as Orlando grabbed his hand truck like a partner and together, danced off toward his destination.

Oblivious to the hustle and bustle surrounding him, the musical elf belted rap lyrics as he bopped his way around conveyors, down an exit ramp, through a utility door and into the maze of corridors leading to the various stockrooms.

Still trapped inside the stockroom holding Cleosistah, Austen could hear Orlando's voice echoing through the corridors and tiptoed towards the door. She motioned with her finger for Cleosistah to be quiet and sat the doll down gently against the wall. Austen placed her ear against the oak door, closed her eyes and held her breath, concentrating on the muffled echo. Unable to make out anything through the thick wood, she lay on the floor and leaned her ear close to the spacious crack under the door.

From her new vantage point, the voice was not only clearer, it was now accompanied by the intermittent squeak of the hand truck's wheels. Both grew louder until they reached their peak on the other side of the door and stopped. Austen shifted her head, peeked under the door and saw the edge of red-soled shoes stepping in rhythm. This was definitely not Christmas Past. The rapping started up again, interspersed with the sound of jangling keys. Whoever it was, they were about to enter the stockroom.

Austen jumped up and hid behind one of the many boxes strewn about the room after her fall. She ducked low and quieted her breathing under the sound of a key inserted into the iron lock, twisted then removed. After a few moments, she heard the keys jangle again and the lock retried with no success. Between attempts, Austen peeked over the lid of the box, readjusting her position and the boxes around her for a view of the person entering.

Austen suddenly noticed the open box from which she took Cleosistah sitting steps away from the door. Its flaps lay open awaiting discovery. She listened intently for the gangling of keys that signaled failure, then darted from her hiding place just as another was inserted into the lock. She quickly stuffed the packing material into the box then turned for Cleosistah. She froze in her tracks at the sound of the key successfully turned. The door would open any second now. Unable to grab Cleosistah or run back to her hiding spot, she quickly stepped into the box and pulled the flaps inward as best she could, a moment before Orlando pushed the door open wide squeezing the seated Cleosistah against the wall and activating her voice.

"Do you know any games we could play?" asked Cleosistah.

Fortunately for Austen, Orlando could barely hear his own thoughts over the ear buds planted deep in his ears. Standing directly over the box containing the stowaway, Orlando read the ticket from the light entering through the open door. Austen's curiosity nearly got the best of her. She wanted to see what an elf really looked like up close and peered through the opening in the flaps, but Orlando only offered her intermittent flashes of green and red as he matched the stock code on the side of the box with the ticket between dance moves.

With the contents verified, he taped the lid shut, sealing Austen inside and placed another box on top. Had he been more attentive to his job, he may have questioned the extra weight as he slid the blade of his hand truck underneath the boxes, but time was of the essence. Though a slacker in every sense, even he realized the consequences of being the one responsible for delaying the Sleigh's launch. Finding the correct key to unlock the stockroom door had cost him precious time. He was determined to make it up on his return trip.

He wheeled the packages out, pulled the door shut and took off at sprinters pace through the winding corridors. Back on the main floor, he darted in, out and around machinery and personnel as he retraced his meandering path. Now within sight of his destination, he took the next corner with breakneck speed and skidded to a halt at the sight of the Ghost of Christmas Past standing inches in front of him.

Like an enlisted man confronted by his commanding officer for a snap inspection, Orlando immediately snapped to attention, held his breath and snatched the ear buds from his ears. The shrill music blasted through the mini microphones and forced him to quickly place his iPod on pause under her withering stare. He could tell by her stance that she was in no mood for delay by anyone or anything (not that she ever was), and quickly pulled his cargo to the side, clearing a path for the stern ghost. He dared not look at her openly kept his eyes lowered as she dismissed him with a derisive snort.

He exhaled a sigh of relief the moment she turned the corner with military precision. Rattled by his encounter with the nicknamed 'Ghoul of Christmas Past', he quickly placed both boxes on the conveyor, signed the tickets, and then handed them to Stephen.

"That's the last of it. When those go through, start shutting it down," he ordered.

The box containing Austen traveled down the conveyor. She could hear the hum of machinery and wondered where she was. The cramped space offered her little in the form of movement and desperate to see where she was heading, tried to poke a hole in the corner of the box. However, it was too late. The box was spun every which way by the mechanical arms, scanned and gift-wrapped then sent into the transformation chamber for storage on Santa's sleigh.

Austen's wish to escape had been realized, but not in a way she could have ever imagined.

Less than a mile away, the Ghost of Christmas Present also completed preparation for his trip back to the world of humans. Satisfied with his appearance and imminent appointment, he pocketed the itinerary and faded out of his office as the clock turned 11:55.

A moment later, he faded back in, retrieved the handheld device from his desk, and then faded out again.

CHAPTER 22

Arthur stood in his foyer trying to calm his nerves. He felt like a high school freshman asked to the prom by a senior cheerleader. The possibilities that his time with Beverley represented made him question what he was inviting by his actions. Part of him warned that this was a bad idea, but the overwhelming consensus was voting for it. He finally allowed himself to admit that it felt good to feel that feeling about someone again.

Like most children, Austen was a deep sleeper so there was little chance of waking her, nonetheless he tiptoed up the stairs and eased open her door. He did not see her head on the pillow so he opened the door wider allowing the light in the hallway to cast its beam inward.

Her bed was empty.

She must be in the bathroom. He turned towards the door a few steps down the hallway. Even though it was open and the light off, he looked inside anyway.

Curiosity quickly turned to concern. His mind began to invent hopeful scenarios to calm any arising fear. Maybe she had heard him enter and knowing he was coming to check on her, decided to hide and scare him.

He opened her door wide and turned on the lights.

"Hmmm, I see Austen isn't in her bed," he voiced aloud as he crept toward the far side of the bed where her quilt had gathered on the floor. "I wonder where she could be. Maybe she's hiding under . . . here!" He snatched the quilt high hoping to see her smiling face, but only a pair of shoes and a pillow stared back at him.

Concern now turned to fear. He looked under the bed and checked the closet, rifling his arms through her clothes.

He felt his pulse quicken as adrenaline-fueled panic began to attack his senses. He ran frantically through the house calling Austen's name, opening every door and turning on every light in his search. Frustrated, he began to shake with fear.

"Oh God, no!"

Beverley was expecting Arthur to return at any moment with more eggnog. She stood in the kitchen with two fresh glasses each holding a shot of rum when he burst in.

"Austen's gone!"

It took Beverley a moment for his comment to register. The frantic look on his face and the labored breathing told her that he was not joking.

"What?! What do you mean gone? Gone where?"

"I don't know! Gone! She's gone! She not in her bedroom or the bathroom or the -- I searched the whole house and she's gone!"

Arthur's face was a portrait of desperation. Beverley was accustomed to calming first time flyers agitated and even distraught during their first bout with turbulence, but this category of terror was new to her. It was personal. Her close proximity to and relationship with Arthur and Austen made her a victim by association. Arthur's fear unleashed a wellspring of emotion so intense she dropped one of the glasses and barely heard it shatter on the tile floor.

Maybe it came from watching too many crime dramas on television, but somewhere deep in her mind, she knew that time was the essence in missing persons cases. Arthur's uncontrolled tears told her that he had reached his breaking point and needed her untapped strength to guide him. This was no time for reassurance. It was a call to action.

She sprang from her side of the island, grabbed his hand and pulled him behind her as she ran out of the house.

"She has to be here somewhere! Search the house again!" shouted Beverley. "Go upstairs, I'll take downstairs!"

She watched as Arthur tried to take the steps two at a time, his legs failing him as he screamed Austen's name. Since his side of the duplex was exactly opposite to her layout, her search progressed smoothly but she soon found herself silently cursing her thoroughness after looking in places no child could possibly be hiding or God forbid, be placed.

She could hear Arthur's restless footsteps on the ceiling mirroring her path below and within the first minute she realized his initial assessment was correct. Austen was gone.

The sound of his footfall told her that Arthur was heading downstairs. She met him in the kitchen and before he had a chance to speak, issued orders.

"Go look out back, I'll see if she's out front. Go!"

His face brightened at the prospect of the expanded search. In his confused state, he hadn't thought to look out back since the patio doors were still locked from the inside. Nonetheless, he took off in a mad dash to find his child, leaving Beverley to begin her search out front.

The backyard was a small, neatly manicured plot lit by a fluorescent dusk to dawn lamp suspended from the eave of the duplex. Located at the midway point, it provided light to both his and Beverley's backyard. The only features dotting its landscape were a table with two chairs, a bird feeder, birdbath and a small tool shed doubling as storage. A six-foot high wooden fence bordered the yard on three sides and offered little escape for a child except through the gate that opened onto the driveway.

Arthur ran the length of fence looking over into the surrounding yards calling Austen's name. He shook the lock on the shed door and saw that it remained secure. He ran along the stone pavers outlined with colorful Pansies he and Austen had planted just over a month ago through the gate and onto the carport. Though locked, he looked through each window of the car checking to see if for some unknown reason she decided to stow away inside for safety from what he dared not imagine. Not seeing her inside, he looked underneath the vehicle.

He had a view of the street from the driveway and could see Beverley half way down the block searching the shadows of houses and bending every so often to look under cars parked on the street. He realized the only place he had not looked was under the house. The crawl space was just that, a space with a height of no more than three feet. An adult would have to resort to crawling, but a child could easily stoop and navigate their way through. Maybe she knew he had bought her a bicycle for Christmas and wanted to see it.

The cold was beginning to seep into his bones as he ran back into the backyard. He hadn't thought to put on a jacket before searching outdoors. A stiff wind began to blow forcing him to rub his bare arms with his hands to generate temporary warmth.

Out on the street, Beverley was also feeling the cold's bite. The gusty wind, which seemed to come out of nowhere, verified Beverley's suspicion that the temperature was dropping. Like Arthur, she had run out of her house without a coat and was now paying the price. Her thin cotton blouse offered no resistance to the elements. With each step, she felt the cold knife through her. The more her search widened, the more diminished her hopes became.

"I could be out here all night and not locate Austen," she chattered through her teeth.

They were wasting time. Not one to wander off, Austen had obviously been kidnapped and the sooner they contacted the authorities, the sooner they could announce an Amber Alert and find the scared child. The motive for such an act did not cross Beverley's mind. There were enough crazies in the world with motives all their own.

Shivering, Beverley fought her way through the gust but made it a point to continue her search at various intervals in the hopes that she would see something, anything that would lend a clue to Austen's disappearance. Her search had taken her the length of the block in both directions. Now within sight of Arthur's house, she picked up her pace and dashed to get out of the cold just as the wind began to subside.

With the doors of the duplex open, Arthur's foyer provided little relief from the cold outside. Beverley slammed shut the door and grabbed Arthur's jacket from the coat rack. On her tiny frame, the oversized down jacket felt like a warm blanket as she hugged it close to remove the chill.

Arthur must still be out back. Beverley hurried into the kitchen, grabbed the cordless phone from its base on the counter next to the refrigerator and started to dial 911, but decided it best to first tell Arthur of her plans.

She stepped out onto the deck, quickly scanned the yard and called Arthur's name but received no response. Eyeing the open gate, she headed toward the carport to find him. Once again, the wind began to pick up, slamming shut the French doors behind her and forcing the gate to flap violently on its hinges.

She placed her foot against the open gate to steady it and scanned the carport and driveway beyond, shouting over the howling wind.

"Arthur? Arthur? Where are you? We need to call the police!"

Thankfully, the wind began to subside as she waited for a response. Moments later, the stillness returned, making her feel all the more alone. *Where are you, Arthur?* Her breathing deepened, sending clouds of frosty air as the fear knotted in the pit of her stomach.

She looked at the phone and could barely feel her fingers holding it. She decided it was time to call the police with or without Arthur's approval and headed inside to warm her hands. Better to air on the side of caution, after all, Austen may have been missing for nearly an hour. Arthur would understand.

Blowing into her hands and flexing her fingers to restore warmth, she darted inside the house leaving the French doors unlocked in case Arthur decided to use that entrance. She was just about to dial 911 when a shadow of movement in the kitchen entered her periphery.

"Arthur?" Beverley assumed it was he and knowingly hurried to join him. She swung around the edge of the refrigerator and skidded to a halt. Standing in front of her, wearing a red suit and a silly smile was none other than the Ghost of Christmas Present.

CHAPTER 23

Fireworks lit up the clear night sky announcing the moment the immense crowds had waited all day to see. Their anticipation, fueled by pride and alcohol, erupted in a deafening cheer as the massive hangar doors opened revealing Santa's sleigh.

As a tribute to their storied past, a team of eight 'Christmas' reindeer pulled the sleigh with ease toward the launch pad with their powerful haunches. Much larger and stronger than their Lapland cousins, their magnificent racks, polished and decorated with shining bulbs and colorful garland, towered over the crowd as they stepped along the icy path with grace and regal bearing. A fixture of every Christmas festivity, they relished the adoration pouring forth from the crowd and seemed to turn and pose for each flash bulb.

This set of reindeer was the tenth generation descendants of the original eight that had been retired from action more than a century earlier. Much like Budweiser's Clydesdales, they had become indelible symbols of the Christmas brand and were always used in ceremonial processions.

The day after Christmas, Santa hitched the team to his original sleigh and 'flew' invited dignitaries along the parade route to celebrate the end of a successful delivery season. After the parade, anyone wanting to take pictures with the famous animals could visit with them in individual stalls bearing their names and pedigreed history.

There was no 'Rudolph', at least no real live reindeer named Rudolph. He was the official mascot created in response to a steady stream of polls showing that amongst humans Christmas was skewing 'old'. Terms used to describe and promote the holiday like 'traditional' and 'festive' had appealed to parents more than children. In an all out campaign to make the holiday 'younger' and capture the next generation of enthusiasts, 'Rudolph the Red Nosed Reindeer' along with his heroic back-story gave the holiday the boost Christmas Industries needed. So successful was the flying neon-nosed cartoon that soon afterwards, a slew of characters from the Grinch to Frosty the Snowman helped deliver the Christmas message worldwide to children of all ages. This year's ceremonial 'Rudolph' was actually Kris Kringle's nephew, Matthew. He walked ahead of the team with his red nose light flashing and threw candy canes to the crowd.

After the reindeer positioned the sleigh on the launch pad, they were unhitched and the launch pad cleared. The crowd gave voice to the digital countdown and watched as a large red Christmas ornament mounted on the top of the production facility lowered in unison with the countdown. When the clock hit zero, the sleigh let out a blast of steam, began to hover above the pad and in a spectacular burst of light, shot southward into the night sky.

❄ ❄ ❄ ❄ ❄ ❄ ❄

The Ghost of Christmas Past stood outside the door to Austen's storeroom cell and checked her watch. *The Ghost of Christmas Future should have returned with Arthur by now.* She entered the dimly lit storeroom and seeing the crushed and scattered boxes, knew exactly what Austen had attempted. The child's tenacity reminded her of her own determined spirit and drew an appreciative though somewhat annoyed smile of approval.

She stood in the middle of the room and searched the shadows with hooded eyes. Austen was obviously hiding somewhere amidst the boxes. Unfortunately, Christmas Past was in no mood to play 'hide and seek'. Time was of the essence, and she had none to spare.

"Austen, come out from wherever you are." Her commanding voice, filled with authority, resounded in the room. Her patience, already thin as a knife's edge, grew sharper with each passing second she waited for Austen to expose herself.

"Austen! Come out now or else!" she threatened, placing her hands on her fleshy hips while studying the room for any sight or sound of movement.

A rat darted from its hiding space behind a box, scurried across the floor and disappeared under the doorway into the corridor. It was as if it sensed the growing tension and wanted no part of what surely was to come.

The thought that Austen could have escaped did not cross Christmas Past's mind. She had expressly forbid her to do so. Instead, she focused on the fact that she had called Austen's name twice and for whatever reason, the child, and a human one at that, had had the audacity to ignore her. Such feats of insubordination were so far beyond Christmas Past's ability to comprehend, that something was amiss.

Christmas Past closed her eyes and raised her hands as if standing behind an invisible lectern upon which a huge book sat. With Santa on his delivery, she had no reservations about turning back the time in such a limited environment. Like a maestro conducting time, she deftly waved her hands, strumming through the pages of history. The air in the room rippled in obedience turning back time to her tempo and revealed to her the previous happenings taken place.

The rat reentered the room running backwards towards his original hiding place. Soon thereafter Orlando entered and dropped off his packages. After his departure, Past frowned at the sight of Austen emerging from the box. A look of disgust crossed her face as she slammed shut the portal sending forward a tide of activity as time quickly reset itself to the present.

"Foolish child! Now your fate is sealed. No matter, one less human to deal with."

❄ ❄ ❄ ❄ ❄ ❄ ❄

At the sight of Beverley, he straightened, cleared his throat and stated matter-of-factly, "Hello, I am the Ghost of Christmas Present."

Since the unfortunate events of September eleventh had occurred, Sky Trans Airlines had mandated use of air marshalls on all international flights and ordered all of their flight attendants and pilots to complete basic self defense training in an effort to beef up security. As part of their training, they also attended classes focused on reading passengers body language and emotional responses to a variety of stimuli to identify those considered security risks. At the time, many thought the seminars useless but Beverley took them seriously. Now facing what she felt was such a threat, she was glad she did.

A combination of things triggered her response. There was his unexpected appearance, followed by the way he was dressed, his ridiculous introduction stating that he was a ghost, and finally, the way he just stood there, smiling calmly while the world was falling apart around her. Defaulting to her training, she immediately launched into an adrenaline fueled self-defense routine against the stranger while voicing the cadence.

"Kick, scratch, punch, subdue!" she screamed while executing the moves drilled repeatedly into their heads by the instructor.

In his many 'visits' in the past, Christmas Present was privy to the violent tendencies practiced by humans, though he had never actually witnessed any. Now that he was the target of such force, he did not stand a chance. Beverley's actions were far beyond the scope of anything he (or Claire by extension) could have ever anticipated.

Her initial front kick found its target and buried the ball of her foot deep into his solar plexus. He doubled over in pain holding his gut, which placed his face in line to receive a raking scratch across his face. She followed it with an uppercut to his throat that sent him reeling backwards.

"Ghost my ass!" Beverley gritted her teeth and assumed her 'response' position a few feet from his head, ready for another round of assault the moment he showed any sign of retaliation. Shocked that her maneuver had worked so well, she was flooded with a surge of power. Years of high impact aerobic workouts had served her well, making her limber and strong. A part of her *wanted* him to get up. Christmas Present was the physical manifestation of the fear and frustration she felt with Austen's disappearance. Now that she had a chance to strike out against it, the force she unleashed was devastating.

Christmas Present gasped for air as he mustered the strength to rise as far as his knees. The heel of Beverley's right palm to his temple was the reward for his effort, quickly followed by a weak but effective left hook behind his right ear sent him back to the floor. He rolled onto his back moaning as bright spots swam slowly across his line of vision.

Satisfied that she held the upper hand, Beverley backed away keeping her eyes glued on the brightly dressed intruder.

"Don't move! I'm calling the police!"

Christmas Present held up a hand trying to speak but could only manage a guttural moan.

"Don't move!" she warned and began to dial 911. She was about to depress the final 'one' when she literally froze. She could still hear and see perfectly, but for some unknown reason her body refused to respond regardless of how hard she willed movement.

Panic welled up inside and made its presence known through a series of rapid blinks as she watched helplessly as

Christmas Present righted himself and sat rubbing his aching head trying to regain his equilibrium.

"Why did you attack me?" he breathed with difficulty. Using the edge of the island for support, he slowly pulled himself to his feet. "I wasn't going to hurt you," he said while squinting his eyes against the pain racking his body.

Beverley could do nothing but watch in horror as he steadied, then stretched to loosen his aching back, wincing with pain at the sound of a loud pop, which was followed by a series of muffled cracks. Christmas Present shook his head to clear the fog as he made his way delicately toward Beverley, her eyes growing wider with each gingerly step he took.

"I'm sorry about this," he offered while easing the buzzing receiver from her hand. "There's nothing wrong with you, you're just frozen in the moment . . . for my safety." He hung up the phone then faced Beverley with a plea of surrender. "If I release you will you promise to at least listen to me? Blink your eyes if you do."

Beverley fluttered her eyelids. She was not in any pain, but the feeling, or lack of feeling brought on by the spontaneous paralysis was unnerving. She longed for control, if not over the situation then at least over her own body.

"Okay. Now, you promised, so don't do anything or I'll have to freeze you again. Okay?"

Beverley fluttered her eyes again. She was expecting some fancy hand movement or magical words to signal her imminent release, but neither one came. Her reanimation was as unexpected as her freezing. The anticipated force of her sudden ability to move cast her forward into his arms. She recoiled at his touch and pushed him away slapping her arms where he held her as though she had mistakenly stepped into a huge spiders web.

"How did you do that?" she panted. She cautiously eased backwards with baby steps careful not to make any sudden moves lest he take that as an excuse to freeze her again.

"Part of my power allows me to freeze things in the present. I'm sorry," he said, once again holding up his palms in a gesture of peace.

"I didn't want to, but you were going to call the police and possibly hit me again."

There were so many thoughts running through Beverley's head she could hardly focus on one. She suddenly became aware of her hands and noticed that they were shaking uncontrollably. She made fists to quiet them, which made Christmas Present stiffen with fear. Afraid he had taken her action as a sign of promised violence, she quickly loosened her fists and folded her arms tightly across her heaving chest. Her self-imposed straight jacket helped calm her nerves and focus her attention.

"If you're a ghost, how could I hit you?" she asked with a tone of heavy skepticism.

Christmas Present relaxed with the question. Not because he felt as though some semblance of order had been restored or Beverley was showing some sign of trusting him, but because he knew the answer.

"Because I'm the Ghost of Christmas Present, I live in the present which makes me look and feel as real as you. I can't explain it. It just is." He searched her face for any sign of belief, but it was a mask of confusion and uncertainty.

His explanation would have sounded more plausible had Beverley been as familiar with the three spirits as any resident of the North Pole was. Though parameters governing their existence were common knowledge, but the particulars remained shrouded in mystery known only to Santa, and to what extent, no one but he knew.

Much like he, Christmas Past was equally as real to the touch since she was comprised of events that had already happened. However on occasion, she had the ability to appear translucent depending on the viewer's perspective of the past. Though past events were categorized as a series of solid facts, some people remembered things one way, others another way. Time was a prism through which the viewer saw facts as faceted truths depending on their point of view. Christmas Present's reality, when passed on to Christmas Past for storage, should have remained fact, but over the centuries, she had learned how to bend his reality and manipulate its content and context to her advantage. The depth of her delusionary skills was immense, which made her a force to be reckoned with.

Christmas Future was, simply put, an enigma. It was also real but appeared and operated under a cowl of uncertainty. It was always changing. Its form was a function of the many futures possible; defined by choices made in the present. Christmas Past understood Christmas Future best. Often seen together, the adage 'those who choose to forget their past often repeat it,' made her the perfect compliment to Christmas Future's power since she forgot nothing.

Beverley was not sure what to make of Christmas Present's answer. It all sounded like the ramblings of a madman to her. The only thing she knew to be real was that Austen was missing and Christmas Present had frozen her in time. As long as he stayed where he was, she would stall by continuing to ask questions until she got some answers or Arthur returned.

While he was searching her face, she was doing the same. He seemed pleasant and harmless enough but who could say for sure? So much had gone wrong in the past few minutes that she was having difficulty understanding any of it. She was hoping that Arthur would appear as miraculously as Christmas Present did, but with each passing moment assumed he too had met with Austen's fate.

"Where'd you come from? Where are Arthur and Austen? What did you do with them?" she blurted out in one breath.

"Whoa, slow down," begged Christmas Present. He could only process so much at one time. "Who are you?"

"I'm Beverley. I live next door."

"Okay Beverley, nice to meet you. Like I said, I'm the Ghost of Christmas Present."

"You can't be serious," she countered.

Her response shocked Christmas Present. He had never had his identity questioned, or had he? He could not remember. Suddenly, a thought occurred to him.

"I'll prove it," he said reaching into his pocket to pull out his wallet.

Beverley watched with astonishment as he sifted through scraps of paper and cards with the joy of a child preparing to show an interested adult the latest additions to his baseball card collection.

"Here is my Peppermint Plaza security badge, see the address, 2525 Winter Wonderland Parkway, North Pole." He edged closer holding it out front for Beverley to see. She leaned in for a closer look but refused to commit and take a step forward. Seeing her hesitance, he placed it on the island and slid it towards her.

"And here is my bowling league registration, oh, wait a minute!"

He dug deeper into his wallet and proudly produced what he believed would be the final piece of evidence necessary.

"A picture of me with Santa Claus."

This, Beverley had to see. He offered the picture at arms length. She edged closer and snatched it from him. She was expecting a posed picture of he and some mall Santa, but instead it showed he and a corporate-looking gentleman standing in his office with his arm around Christmas Present's shoulder. Both shared a hold on a plaque as though standing for a photo op during an awards ceremony.

Beverley's only reference to Santa Claus was the standard one; a fat, red suited old man with a huge white beard. This man in the picture was a vision of health and vitality and wore a well-tailored suit. The only feature he shared with her view of Santa was his white mustache and beard.

"Is this supposed to be Santa Claus? The real Santa Claus?"

"The one and only," verified Christmas Present with a proud smile.

Beverley stared at the photo, then at the other forms of ID Christmas Present had presented. She tossed them back on the table thoroughly unconvinced. Whatever fear she had experienced dissipated with the rationalization that he was not dangerous, at least not to her . . . but maybe to himself. He was obviously suffering from some sort of delusional fixation on the Christmas season. There were assisted-living homes located at both ends of the block. Maybe he was an outpatient from some mental institution that was off his meds and had wandered in from the streets after hearing her calling Austen's name. In a way, she felt sorry for him. On any other day, she may have tried to help him. Chances were there were people looking for him as ardently as she was searching for Austen. The only question still tugging at her mind was how he was able to 'freeze' her.

Christmas Present frowned at her response. He picked up his identification, returned it to his wallet and stuck it inside his jacket pocket. Suddenly, the silly smile reappeared. He pulled out a folded sheet of paper and waved it for Beverley to see.

"What's that?" she inquired.

"Proof my dear," he said unfolding the paper. "This is Austen's letter she wrote to Santa Claus and the reason I am here."

A look of intrigue flashed across Beverley's face.

"He gave it to me. It seems her Christmas spirit has been ruined by her father, a Mr. Arthur Fisher, so I'm here to have a little chat with him."

Beverley took Austen's letter and read it, then looked at the notes placed there along with the 'Urgent Review' stamp. Afterwards, she closed her eyes and shook her head. She did not know how much more of this she could handle.

"Do you know where Mr. Fisher is?" asked Present checking his watch. "The Ghost of Christmas Past should have already come and gone and the Ghost of Christmas Future will be here precisely at one. I don't have much time and we have a lot of ground to cover."

"You mean to tell me you're the Ghost of Christmas Present like in 'A Christmas Carol'."

"Exactly! You know Charles Dickens too?" asked Christmas Present innocently.

Beverley could not believe what she was hearing. She leaned against the island and began massaging her temples. The twinge of a headache was starting to surface.

"I must be dreaming like Arthur was. He was right, this feels so real," she said to herself.

"What dream? Mr. Fisher had a dream about me."

Beverley nodded. "He said he had a dream and some rich guy, kind of like when Jacob Marley appeared to Scrooge, warned him that three spirits were going to visit."

"Where is Mr. Fisher now, do you know?" asked Christmas Present with growing concern.

"No. Austen is missing and we went to look for her. Now he's gone and I - I don't know what . . . I don't know what happened to them. They're both gone." Beverley's voice trailed off. She felt tears begin to well in her eyes. Unease crossed Christmas Present's brow. He felt her anguish and approached softly, pulling out a stool for her to sit on.

"Maybe you ought to have a seat and tell me everything that's happened so far tonight."

CHAPTER 24

Minutes after the last letter had been processed and its request approved, Santa's timetable was plotted by mission control. The names and addresses of fortunate children were uploaded and the most efficient route charted and programmed into the GPS unit hardwired to the sleigh's automatic cruise control. Like most captains on efficiently run vessels with experienced crews, Santa had very little to do except sit back, monitor the progress and enjoy the ride.

Contrary to popular belief, gifts were not delivered to each home exactly at midnight. Even in their hyper-light delivery mode, it was impossible to meet such a schedule. Instead, they started deliveries at the northernmost point of the first time zone to hit midnight. The sleigh then followed the pre-plotted route that ended at the southernmost point of the time zone at one o'clock. As midnight struck the next time zone to the west, they reversed course and starting at the southern edge, delivered gifts until completion in the northern reaches at one o'clock. The zigzagging route from north to south to north again and all points in between was repeated over the course of an entire earth day. By the time the mission was completed, the sleigh would log nearly half a million miles, enough to circumnavigate the globe twenty-five times.

It may sound like this made for a busy schedule, but the majority of the earth's surface was covered by water and its inhabitants concentrated in relatively small areas. This meant the trip was dominated by travel time and punctuated with hectic moments of activity over well-populated areas like the United States and Europe where the Christmas tradition held sway.

The weather forecasted by Chip, the meteorologist, was accurate as always. The next stop on the sleigh's journey called for heavy snow to coat rooftops with a thick blanket of dry white powder. Had someone braving the elements looked into the night sky, they would have seen what appeared to be a shooting star streaming across the heavens then disappearing from view. Their view, that is. Santa's sleigh was not only a technological marvel; it was master of the illusionary process.

The sleigh's exterior appeared brilliant red when stared at from a fixed point under light. Closer inspection revealed a layer of clear anti-reflective matte polymer designed to reduce drag and dampen sound. The transparent layer also served to protect the thin sheet of transistorized film coating the sides and bottom serving as a projection screen. It received digital inputs from a series of omni-directional cameras mounted on the roof that continuously recorded the night sky from zenith to horizon and displayed the images on the film.

The result was a disappearing act of sorts. Whether the sky was clear or blanketed with clouds, the exterior display allowed the sleigh to seamlessly blend into its ever-changing environment. Thus, no human could say they had ever seen Santa's sleigh.

Those that happened to stare at the right spot in the night sky at the right time long enough to actually see something usually dismissed it as weather related anomaly. Others vaguely described what they rightly saw as a spaceship from an alien world and faced ridicule trying to convince family and friends that they had actually seen a UFO.

Delivery of the gifts was pure christmasynchronicity. The regeneration unit decoded the digitized matter and reconfigured the gifts in an instant by address. Teams of elves quickly bagged the gifts and passed them along to delivery specialists. Like a finely tuned military attack team, they dropped onto rooftops from the hovering sleigh, and gained access down chimneys or vent pipes to place their precious cargo underneath Christmas trees. Cookies and drinks left for Santa were boxed and bottled for distribution to homeless shelters and food banks.

Street by street and city by city, the sleigh executed its mission flawlessly under the watchful eye of Santa. Ever the perfectionist, his eye scrutinized the process for any deficiency and recorded every detail that could be improved upon. They were delivering more and more gifts each year, and at that pace, needed any and every suggestion to make their operation more efficient.

Six thousand miles to the north, the Ghost of Christmas Past was also keeping a watchful eye. Her's however, were on Arthur. Ironically, he sat in the same chair occupied earlier by Austen in the lab, his hands bound tightly behind him. The last thing he remembered was searching for Austen in his backyard, now he sat staring into the sinister eyes of Christmas Past.

"Where's Austen?" he demanded angrily pulling against his restraints. "I know you took her!"

"How should I know? She's your daughter," mocked Christmas Past. "Had you not abandoned her and placed your interests above your child's, she would be safe at home. I always thought a parent's greatest responsibility was for their child's safety and well-being." She leaned in closer to drive her point home. "It seems you've failed on both fronts. Wouldn't you agree Mr. Fisher?"

Arthur felt a pang of guilt shoot through him. An expert at probing for weakness, Christmas Past could easily manipulate the minds of the strongest of men. In Arthur's confused and remorseful state, he was putty in her hands.

He had no way of knowing that she needed him more than he needed her, which gave Christmas Past the upper hand. His successful exploitation was pivotal if her plans were to succeed. With him here, her schedule was back on track. For it to stay that way, she would have to proceed carefully. The art of interrogation required instilling a certain level of hope in the heart of the interrogated if they were to cooperate fully. Knowing that his hope rest on allaying any fear about Austen's demise, she decided to address it directly.

"To answer your question, Austen is resting comfortably nearby, and if you want to see her, you will do exactly as I say and cooperate fully. Do you understand?" she instructed.

Arthur stared into his lap, determined not to comply until he had some assurance that she was telling him the truth. His tactic did not amuse Christmas Past. She violently grabbed his forehead, pushing it back and forcing him to look her directly in the eyes.

"Do you understand Mr. Fisher," she insisted.

Arthur shifted his gaze and looked into the frightened eyes of Dr. Hamilton cowering against the wall. His face relayed to Arthur the hopelessness of his situation and recommended cooperation.

"Yes. I'll do what you say. Just . . . don't hurt her."

"Me, hurt a child?" said Christmas Past releasing her grip. "I would never do that. However, as for you . . . " She let her threat dangle in the air as she stepped back straightening her lace gloves.

"We haven't been properly introduced. I am the Ghost of Christmas Past. And that," she said pointing to a spot behind him, "is the Ghost of Christmas Future."

Arthur craned his neck to see who was standing behind him. From the corner of his eye he could barely make out the semi-translucent red cowl.

"Ghosts?" he chuckled.

His amusement brought a slight smile to Christmas Past's face.

"You laugh. Why is that? Because ghosts don't exist?"

Christmas Past, still smarting from Dr. Hamilton's emboldened stand and Austen's escape, made it a point not to take anything for granted. Curious as to why Arthur was not at home when Christmas Future had arrived earlier, she had looked into his recent past while waiting for Future to return and found what she was looking for.

A sound familiar to Arthur began to fill the cavernous lab. He looked around to find the source of the metallic scraping that grew louder with each passing second. When he looked back at Christmas Past, she had turned into Ernest Anthony Bell III dragging his chains.

"Why do you doubt your senses?" she asked in the same haunting voice.

Since their initial encounter, Ernest's features had rapidly deteriorated. His partially maggot eaten flesh revealed skeletal parts of his anatomy. Arthur shuddered and closed his eyes at the ghastly sight. The sound of Christmas Past's laughter forced him to open them.

"Spiritless man, do you believe in me or not?" she mused.

"There has to be some kind of mistake."

Her face quickly shed the pretense of laughter and twisted into a mask of scorn. "The only mistake was made by you! Your past actions and attitudes towards Christmas has qualified you to participate in a clinical trial of sorts."

Arthur's mind raced to comprehend the meaning of her words. For the first time since his arrival, he looked around the lab and surveyed its contents. The platforms of chemicals, caged animals, copious unintelligible mathematical and chemical formulas on the chalkboards along with Dr. Hamilton standing in a rumpled lab coat told him Christmas Past's use of the word 'clinical' was accurate. He was a lab rat.

"What are you going to do to me?" he asked anxiously.

"Did you know that more humans commit suicide during the Christmas holidays than at any other time of the year? Imagine that. Committing such an act of desperation at a time meant to celebrate life and all it has to offer." She paced the floor like a college professor lecturing her only student. "What if there existed a magic elixir that could cure their depression and make them feel like a child on Christmas morning? Wouldn't that be wonderful?"

By now, Arthur was used to the rapid mood shifts and knew they offered no clue to what she was thinking. On the other hand, his emotions were so transparent that when he grasped the connection between her portrayal of Ernest Bell combined with her use of the words 'suicide' and 'clinical trial', he gasped in horror.

"You killed him! He didn't commit suicide, you killed Ernest Bell!"

"Well done Mr. Fisher quite observant of you. However, I cannot take credit for that. I did not kill him. The fall did. Better yet, the sudden stop did him in. He jumped on his own volition though I admit his motivation was . . . borrowed."

Arthur's demeanor changed with her confession. He exhaled heavily and slumped in his chair as if the weight of her assertion straddled his shoulders. Once again, he locked eyes with Dr. Hamilton confirming his judgment.

"So I guess I'm your new lab rat. You're going to do to me what you did to him."

"Let's hope not," she countered.

"Can I see Austen first?" asked Arthur. His eyes were sad and he suddenly felt very tired. Christmas Past would have pitied him had she been familiar with the emotion. Preparing an optimal subject on which to administer her potion was her only interest and she nodded approval at Arthur's docile compliance. A serene subject would give her the best opportunity to judge the effects of the experiment.

"As soon as we're finished, not only will you be able to see her, you can both return home and enjoy Christmas with a new found zeal the holiday season deserves." she reassured.

She motioned Dr. Hamilton to bring the formula. Anticipating her call, he shuffled forward and awaited her command.

"What's that?" asked Arthur.

"Just a little something the good chemist has been kind enough to prepare. I call it, 'Eau de Christmas Spirit'."

Dr. Hamilton positioned the nozzle inches from Arthur's nose.

"What's it going to do to me?"

"It's going to help you . . ." she began to sing, *"Have yourself, a merry little Christmas . . ."*

Dr. Hamilton squeezed the atomizer releasing a small scented cloud of dazzling liquid that hung in the air like a rainbow colored mist. Arthur instinctively turned his head and tried to hold his breath, but that only resulted in his inhaling most of the cloud when he gasped for air.

"Let your heart be light . . ." sang Christmas Past.

A wash of warmth flowed through Arthur. He relaxed and breathed deep, pulling in the last of the lingering mist.

"From now on, your troubles will be out of sight . . ."

A smile crossed his lips as he leaned back, closed his eyes and let the world drift away as he began savoring the euphoria that now held him in its sweet embrace.

CHAPTER 25

"And then both of them were gone. So I decided the best thing to do was call the police. That's when I ran in here and saw you," finished Beverley.

"Uhm-hmn, okay," said Christmas Present. He was feverishly taking notes. "You're right, that is strange. What was your name again?"

"Beverley!" Frustrated, she stood and shouted at him. "Geez, how many times are you going to ask me that?"

The question clearly embarrassed Christmas Present. He lowered his head, shrinking like a child publicly disciplined by a parent. Beverley immediately regretted her outburst. She sighed, sat down and placed an apologetic hand on his shoulder.

"I'm sorry. I didn't mean that," she said in a softer tone. "It's just that I'm really frustrated and scared and nobody seems to have any answers."

Christmas Present accepted her apology with a nod.

"I need to tell you something."

"What?"

"I suffer from a . . . condition of sorts."

Beverley shifted to face him. He nervously rubbed his hands on his thighs and closed his eyes as if searching for the right words to convey his secret.

"What is it?" she asked fearfully.

"Since I live in the present, I don't really have a past." He peered into her eyes for any indication that she was following him before continuing.

"Okay, I'm with you so far . . . I think."

"I mean I have one, we all do, but mine is different. It's sort of on loan to, no that's not it . . . it belongs to her. See as soon as the present becomes the past, it goes directly to her."

His convoluted hand gestures meant to illustrate his narration were not doing much to help Beverley understand him.

"Well not directly, it usually takes a few minutes, but after that, it's hers. She has total recall to it and can access it anytime she needs it no matter how small the detail. I'm telling you, she's like a walking file cabinet."

Beverley threw up her hands in exasperation.

"Her? Her who and what is this 'it' she gets? Arthur and Austen are missing, I'm trying to figure out what's going on, and you're sitting here babbling like the village idiot!"

For the second time, Beverley had to offer her apology.

"I'm sorry. Go on, I'm listening. It's just a little confusing."

"I agree, it is. Because I live in the present . . . I'm a little short on memory."

"How short?"

"I don't know, anywhere from one to five minutes. Some things I can remember, others it depends on how stressed I am . . . I think. And to tell you the truth, I'm kind of stressed right now . . . ahhh --"

"Beverley."

"Beverley," he repeated, writing it down this time. "B-E-V-E-R-L -- Do you spell Beverley with an 'L-Y' or 'L-E-Y'?"

Beverley caught herself before saying something she would have to apologize for yet again. Instead of snapping, she clenched her fists, leaned against the island and exhaled a deep sigh.

Meanwhile, just south of the Canadian border, the sleigh hovered over another neighborhood preparing to make a delivery. As usual, the process of reconfiguring, sorting and bagging gifts continued unabated. Elves grabbed their assignments, leaped onto rooftops and miraculously compressed or elongated to fit into whatever opening was available for silent entry.

Richie, better known to his comrades as 'Roto-Richie' for his uncanny ability to quickly snake down the most complicated of entryways, was a veteran delivery specialist with more than forty 'southern runs' under his belt. He was Santa's top deliveryman, distributing gifts to more households that any other Elf the past five years in a row. The sight of a standard one-pipe chimney made him laugh. He would be back on board, reloaded and off on another delivery before anyone else, thereby increasing his already substantial lead.

The instant he hit the rooftop, he sprang onto the chimney and leaped down the pipe holding his bag overhead. He suddenly felt his descent halted, leaving him suspended in mid-air. His bag was apparently stuck somewhere above him. This had never happened to him before. He jerked his body, tugging at the bag's handle to dislodge the obstruction, but it refused to yield.

Climbing back up the chimney shaft, he pushed the bag upward, climbed out onto the rooftop and decided on another approach. He would drop the bag in first, and then use his weight to force it downward. Of the three gifts inside his bag, the first two entered neatly, but the last and largest of the gifts refused to compress. Regardless of how he manipulated or angled it, it simply would not fit.

Dismayed, he scratched his head and voiced into his headset, "Little Green Four to Big Red One . . . we have a problem."

❋ ❋ ❋ ❋ ❋ ❋ ❋

"I need to call my secretary. She should be able to shed some light on this," concluded Christmas Present.

He stood and felt his pockets, then reached inside each searching for his handheld device.

"What are you looking for," asked Beverley.

"My phone, I'm pretty sure I had it with me when I arrived," he said looking around the kitchen counters and island top.

Beverley joined in the search and noticed the device sitting on the floor where Christmas Present lay after she attacked him.

"There it is," she pointed out.

Christmas Present picked it up and saw the screen cracked in two places. He tried to turn it on but the device was useless.

"Awh, man," he moaned.

"What's wrong?

"My phone is broken. She's going to kill me."

Beverley winced at the assessment and silently cursed herself.

"It's okay you can say it," she partly confessed.

"Say what?"

"That it's my fault. It probably broke when you fell after I hit you."

"You hit me?" His puzzled expression revealed a genuine ignorance about what had taken place earlier. "Why would you do that?"

"Did I say hit? I meant slip," she corrected. "It probably broke when you slipped and fell. Remember?"

She tried her best to paint a look of innocent optimism on her face. He considered her explanation and accepted it verbatim.

"That makes sense. It would explain this knot on the back of my head."

Anxious to move on and change the subject just in case he started to remember what had actually happened, she blurted out, "What are we going to do now? We've got to find them!" By now she was convinced Arthur had met with the same fate as Austen.

"Just relax. I'll head back to the North Pole, talk with my secretary, and find out what's going on. I'm sure there's a simple explanation for all of this. Okay?"

"Okay. What do you want me to do?"

"Just wait here until I return."

"Uh-uhn! I'm not staying here by myself," shrieked Beverley, fearful of being alone in a place that had already claimed two victims. "I'm coming with you!"

"You can't do that. I can't bring a human to the North Pole!"

"Why not?" she demanded, stepping closer to limit his ability to evade her question.

"Because . . . I don't know. There has to be a reason. I just probably forgot what it was."

"Well until you remember what it is, you are not going anywhere without me," she confirmed with a poke to his chest. The look of astonishment on his face at her demand told Beverley that his decision was arbitrary at best. She decided to make it law. "I bet you can't even remember who you're looking for."

"Yes I can," he countered regaining his composure.

"Who then? Who are you looking for? What are their names?" she pressed.

"I'm looking for . . . I have it right here," he said smugly, tapping his jacket pocket. He reached in and pulled out a small stack of index cards with post-it notes of various colors attached to them. Before he could read them, Beverley snatched the stack from his hand and stuffed them inside her bra.

"Hey, give me those!" he demanded indignantly.

"Only if you promise to take me with you. Besides, you need me to help you find them. You don't even know what they look like."

She had him right where she wanted and they both knew it. He snorted his displeasure before stubbornly yielding.

"Alright, alright. I'll take you. But if Santa finds out about this and says anything, I'll tell him you forced me."

"There's a real Santa Claus?"

"I should hope so," he scoffed. "He's my boss. By the way, you may want to grab a jacket and put on some warm shoes. It gets a little cool this time of year."

CHAPTER 26

 As Arthur drifted in and out of consciousness, Dr. Hamilton monitored his heart rate, breathing, blood pressure and eye dilation.

"Well Doctor," requested Christmas Past impatiently.

"It appears to be working, ma'am," said Dr. Hamilton as he unstrapped the blood pressure cuff and pulled the stethoscope from his ears. "The effects of the drug are beginning to show. What we are witnessing is synaptic response to the stimulant. It is duping brain chemistry into synthesizing inordinate amounts of endorphins, resulting in a virtual sensory experience consistent with your stated expectations."

"Will it be permanent?"

"No, ma'am. The control dosage administered was just enough to induce temporary euphoria. Greater systemic exposure will achieve prolonged states and from early indications . . . a rapid addiction," he added with a timbre of regret.

"Excellent!" clapped Christmas Past. "You may yet live long enough to die of old age."

Arthur finally opened his eyes and grinned broadly.

"Merry Christmas, Mr. Fisher," extended Christmas Past after untying his hands. "How does it feel to have a little Christmas Spirit?"

Arthur could not contain his joy. Dr. Hamilton backed away as he leaped from his seat and began prancing about the lab. Perhaps because he had watched 'A Christmas Carol' at least twice every year since his youth, he voiced the same words used by Ebenezer Scrooge the morning of his emancipation.

"I'm as light as a feather, happy as an angel, merry as a schoolboy, and giddy as a drunk! Merry Christmas to everybody and a happy New Year to all the world!"

"Do you know who and where you are?"

"My name is Arthur Fisher and other than that, I really don't care! It's Christmas!"

The entire delivery team stood looking at the wrapped gift that refused to fit down the chimney. Santa knelt and inspected the outside then stroked his beard.

"Hmmm, this is a first. Whom is this gift slated for?"

Carlton, the delivery supervisor anticipated the question and read aloud from a card posted on his clipboard.

"Leslie Gabrielle, age five, sir."

"What's inside?"

"One Cleosistah, a life-sized talking doll, sir."

"That's a new item," Santa noted with a furrow of his brow. "Is this the first one we've delivered?"

"No, sir. We've delivered thirty-five so far. Eighteen by vents and seventeen by chimney."

Santa stood, his face mirroring the puzzlement felt by all. "I suppose the best thing to do is open it up. Maybe something in the way it was packed is causing the problem. If I have to, I'll walk it in personally. Make a note to have diagnostics run on the digitizer when we get back."

"Yes, sir," said Carlton. He anticipated this request as well and immediately handed the completed paperwork to Santa for his signature as the box was opened.

No sooner had Richie pulled back the flaps than Austen's head popped up.

Everyone gasped in awe at the sight of the little girl inside. She in turn gasped at the sight of so many elves staring at her. Santa cleared a path to see what held everyone dumbfounded and was equally as astonished.

"Austen Fisher? Is that you?"

Her eyes grew even wider at her latest gawker. "Yes. Are you Santa Claus?"

"Yes, I am."

"The real Santa Claus?"

"The one and only," he reassured her. "I think we've found the glitch," he said to Carlton then lifted Austen from the box. "Call in and have a replacement sent out ASAP. Continue with the deliveries while I have a word with my little friend here."

"Yes, sir," responded Carlton, already on the phone.

Austen continued to stare at the elves over Santa's shoulder as he carried her toward the front of the sleigh. After clearing a spot where they could sit privately, he took a seat and sat her on his knee.

"Sweetheart, are you okay?" He brushed her hair with his hand and straightened her pajama top.

"Yes."

"What are you doing here? How did you get in that box?"

"I hid in there."

"Yes, but what were . . . where did you . . . let's start at the beginning, shall we? How did you get to the North Pole? Do you remember and can you tell me?"

"Yes, but don't you have presents to deliver?"

"Don't you worry about that," he reassured her. "I have all the help I need delivering gifts tonight. What is important right now is you try to remember everything that happened to you today so I can figure out how a sweet little girl like you ended up on my sleigh. Okay?"

"Okay."

"But first, let's get you something to eat. You must be hungry."

"A little," she answered.

"How about some milk and cookies? I eat yours every Christmas, so why don't you try some of mine, I baked them myself. After that you can tell me everything, okay."

"Okay." Austen smiled with delight and hugged his neck. Santa realized that after her ordeal, she did not intend to release her grip, so he managed as best he could to prepare her snack from his personal lunchbox.

As he watched her eat, he was struck by the steely resolve behind her eyes, and then he remembered the contents of her letter. At some point before the night was over, she would ask and he would have to answer one of the most difficult questions ever posed to him by a child, or for that matter, an adult.

❋ ❋ ❋ ❋ ❋ ❋ ❋

As a flight attendant, Beverley had traveled the world and visited some exotic locations, but the North Pole? This was Shangri-La, El Dorado and the lost city of Atlantis all rolled into one.

Moments after Christmas Present had agreed to take her with him, she had darted out of Arthur's house, changed clothes, put on some wool lined boots, a down filled jacket, fixed her make-up and straightened her hair in the time it would take to microwave a bag of popcorn.

"This jacket look warm enough to you?" she asked Christmas Present.

"That should do."

"Alright, how do we do this?"

"Hmmm . . . I'm not sure. I don't think I've done this before," said Christmas Present. Clueless in such matters, he was open to any suggestion she may have had. Beverley opted for the only reference that seemed to fit the scenario.

"In 'A Christmas Carol', the Ghost of Christmas Past touched Scrooge over his heart to transport him back in time. Maybe that's how you do it," she proposed.

"Okay. Let's try that."

A veteran of the airways, Beverley suddenly felt like a first-time flyer just before takeoff. She closed her eyes and took deep breaths to calm her nerves, unsure of what the experience promised.

She felt Christmas Present's light touch over her heart, followed by a rush of wind that made her close her eyes even tighter. Soon thereafter, the wind subsided and she anticipated the feel of cold air from the North Pole as well as Christmas Present's voice telling her they had arrived safely.

After a few moments, she heard nothing and wondered if she was transporting in some sort of vacuum or portal that nullified all sound and feeling. Perhaps, they were floating in space with the world turning beneath them as so many scenes beamed back to earth from the space shuttle. Curiosity got the better of her and against better judgment, she peeked open an eye only to see that she was still standing in Arthur's kitchen. Christmas Present, on the other hand, had disappeared.

"Present? Christmas Present? Where are you?" she shouted.

The brisk breeze filling the kitchen quickly answered her question and brought Christmas Present to rest in front of her as before.

"Sorry about that. Any other ideas?"

"Yeah, let's try this." She wrapped her arms around him tightly. "Okay, let's go."

The last words she heard were Christmas Present's warning "Hang on tight," before the wind noise drowned everything out.

Moments later, the intertwined travelers faded from view.

CHAPTER 27

Arthur was seated in the center of the lab. A single overhead light fixture illuminated his position and formed a hard circle of light around him. Framed by darkness, the scene was a cliché from every bad B-movie interrogation.

The full effect of withdrawal from 'Christmas Spirit' was beginning to take its toll. He squirmed and fidgeted uneasily trying to decide whether he felt hot or cold as though his body hung suspended under a giant bathroom hand dryer. Though he was beginning to sweat under the heat of the overhead lamp, his mouth remained dry. He worked his lips like an alcoholic to generate even the slightest amount of saliva to moisten his tongue and lips.

"I can see the sample of 'Christmas Spirit' is wearing off," informed Christmas Past. "So before we conclude our business, I need to know about its effectiveness if I am to declare this clinical trial a success."

Arthur looked around to see where she was standing. Like a walking metaphor, he could see her feet slowly tracing the perimeter, perfectly balanced between light and the endless darkness beyond.

"I will be asking you a series of questions, please answer them as quickly and succinctly as possible."

"Can I get another whiff of --"

"Shut up!" She said sternly. "Do you understand?"

"Yes," he answered listlessly.

"What is your daughters name?"

"Austen."

"What day is it?"

"Christmas."

"Where are you?"

"The North Pole."

"And how do you think my 'Christmas Spirit' will be received by your kind?"

Still partially under the effects of the drug, the mere mention of its name caused him to perk up. "They're going to go crazy. I can't wait to tell my friends about how wonderful it made me feel."

Pleased by his testimony, Christmas Past stepped into the circle of light for the first time and faced him.

"And what would you say if I told you that Santa would rather die than let humans have 'Christmas Spirit'?"

"I'd say he was a fat, selfish jerk who deserves to die if he won't let us have any Christmas Spirit."

Christmas Past flashed a fiendish smile at his response. Signaling his ordeal was nearing an end, she lovingly stroked his head and motioned Dr. Hamilton to fetch him a cool drink.

"I couldn't agree with you more, my friend. I couldn't agree with you more."

❋ ❋ ❋ ❋ ❋ ❋ ❋

After hearing Austen's tale, Santa buried his face in his hands and slowly massaged his forehead. Her story was as mesmerizing as it was unbelievable and spoke to a level of dishonesty and duplicity so complete, he could hardly believe it. He stared into space trying to remember if he had witnessed any incident or overheard any snippet of conversation that could have alerted him. Unable to recall any such moment, he silently cursed his inability to discover the conspiracy.

"Did you happen to overhear who Christmas Past sent Christmas Future to get?"

"No sir," said Austen, disappointed that she could not be more helpful. Even she could tell her story troubled him and that he was trying to put on his best face for her benefit.

"Austen, you are as brave as you are beautiful," he said stroking her cheek. "We'll be delivering gifts in your neighborhood soon. I'd better get you home before your father starts worrying about you."

"Did you get me what I asked for?" she asked cheerfully, her face flushed with eagerness.

Santa's face dropped for a bit, then regained an optimistic smile.

"It's not polite to ask or tell someone what you got them for Christmas. You'll have to wait and see when you wake up tomorrow morning, okay."

"Okay!" Her smile contained a trust that sent a spike of agony through Santa.

"Why don't you ride up front with me? Would you like that?"

"Yes!" screeched Austen. "Can I pet the reindeer?"

"We don't use reindeer to drive the sleigh anymore," answered Santa as he led her toward the cockpit.

"You don't? Why not?" Her voice whined with disappointment.

"Animal rights activists made us retire them." He lifted her into the seat and began securing her seat belt. "These days, we use good old fashioned horse power."

"How do you keep from getting lost if Rudolph isn't guiding your sleigh?"

"GPS technology, my dear. Where would we be without it?"

Beverley opened her eyes onto a barren, frozen landscape. Though blustery and bleak, it was a bit warmer than she anticipated. Having departed in the middle of night, the sunlight's bright glare reflecting off the sheets of ice made her squint.

"Are we here? Is this it?" asked Beverley.

Her tone voiced disappointment. Like Austen, she had imagined a magical setting reminiscent of Dorothy's Oz, but this icy tundra was straight from the pages of National Geographic magazine. She released her hold on Christmas Present, then instinctively grabbed him at the sight of a single filed line of emperor penguins silently marching by, totally oblivious to their recently arrived guests.

"Oh, dear," murmured Christmas Present.

"What's that supposed to mean? What's wrong?"

"Uh, nothing," he replied sheepishly.

Beverley was familiar with his non-committal response having heard it enough from her nephews and nieces. They used it when trying to evade responsibility for some act without actually lying about it. She released her hold and looked him squarely in the eyes.

"What do you mean nothing?"

His guilty smile and shrug informed her that something was definitely wrong. As if answering by proxy, the last of the penguins faced Beverley, flapped its tiny wings, squawked and then waddled away. Its explanation could not have been any clearer had she been Dr. Doolittle.

"Christmas Present? I may be mistaken, but don't penguins live on Antarctica . . . the South Pole?"

He answered her by inhaling deeply then exhaling a frosty sigh.

"We're lost, aren't we?""

The Ghost of Christmas Past pushed the melancholy Arthur inside the same storeroom that once held Austen. With the sleigh's departure, production had ceased and she no longer worried that anyone would venture inside and inadvertently liberate him. Besides, he would only be there for a short time if all went according to her plans.

"Have a seat, Mr. Fisher. I have some other business to attend to after which you will --"

"You said I could see Austen," he interrupted.

"Trust me, you will be joining her soon."

She slammed the door shut, locked it behind her and looked down at the waiting Sebastian.

"We are past the point of no return. You know what to do with this," she presupposed handing him a small folded envelope.

"Yes, ma'am," he answered with a resolute nod.

"Good. You must hurry, we have a tight schedule to keep and can't afford any more delays."

"Yes, ma'am." She watched him speed off, then headed in the other direction.

CHAPTER 28

After a few more unscheduled stops, one taking them to the dense jungles of Cambodia and another just feet away from the rim of an active volcano in the South Pacific, the Ghost of Christmas Present and Beverley finally arrived unscathed, though flustered, at the North Pole.

"Much better," breathed Christmas Present in relief. "C'mon, I work in that building over there," he said pointing toward Peppermint Plaza, the home of Christmas Industries.

Christmas Present marched forward leaving Beverley to gawk at the towering icy structures like an Iowa farmhand visiting New York City for the first time. She could not take her eyes off the beautiful buildings rising out of the ground at odd angles like crystalline growths that seemed to defy gravitational logic and violate every architectural standard known to mankind.

Christmas displays magically hovered above the avenue like invisibly tethered hot air balloons. The intermittent curtains of Northern lights snaking across the night sky reflected off the buildings and streets making everything seem alive with movement.

"Omigod!" mouthed Beverley in awe, spinning in every direction trying to see everything at once. "Look at that. It's so pretty. Wow! Oh my goodness. This is incredible."

Temporarily satisfied with her initial intake of the view, she searched for any sign of inhabitants to complete her survey.

"Where is everyone? I want to meet an elf!"

At first, Christmas Present was at a loss and then noticed a billboard boldly declaring the answer. "Everyone's at the annual Christmas Eve celebration. They're waiting for Santa's sleigh to return."

Disappointed by the news, Beverley ran to catch up with him. Though temporarily distracted by the realization that she was indeed in the North Pole, home to Santa Claus, the reason she was there was not lost on Beverley. With each step, she grew more hopeful that they would find out what had happened to Arthur and Austen and somehow rejoin them in time to witness the return of Santa and join in the celebration.

"Christmas Industries," noted Beverley as they entered the expansive lobby filled with the largest poinsettia plants she had ever seen. The leaves flaunted every color in the rainbow and the blooms were fragrant and larger than a dinner plate.

"So this is where you work? Where's your office?"

"This way," answered Christmas Present confidently, heading toward the elevators. He remembered that much. Unfortunately, there was no elevator attendant waiting to corral and redirect his path inside. Instead, he strode by the bank of closed doors and continued on a meandering path that eventually circled the first floor bringing them past the point they entered. He would have continued merrily onto a second lap had Beverley not interceded.

"Uh, Christmas Present?"

"Yes?"

"Your office is on the 112th floor," she said pointing at the wall-mounted directory.

"112th floor?" he questioned, then immediately acknowledged, "That's right."

You are a piece of work. Beverley locked her arm in his and escorted him towards the bank of waiting elevators.

With Beverley leading the way, they quickly found his office.

"Nice digs," she noted. "Corner office, oak desk, nice leather chair and a wall full of awards." She picked up the nameplate on his desk and read it aloud, "The Ghost of Christmas Present, Director of Human Relations. Wow. You're the real deal. A corporate bigwig," she confirmed while he went through his usual routine to gain recognition of his office.

"Omigod!" exclaimed Beverley with the discovery of his windows' panoramic view of the North Pole. Like every human, she had imagined a cozy hamlet filled with happy little people, but had dismissed that stereotype moments after arrival. From the view she now enjoyed, the sheer size and scale of industry rivaled that of the largest metropolitan areas known to man and made her jaw drop.

Standing there looking out onto terrain no human eyes had ever witnessed, she suddenly felt like Neil Armstrong stepping onto the barren landscape of the moon. However unlike the moon, which was visible to human eyes, this place existed beyond the realm of human awareness. Part of her wanted to take a picture and share it with the world, but she knew that was impossible. Their success lie in their anonymity, and any desire on her part to expose that for personal pleasure or gain would destroy the community they had painstakingly created, not to mention Christmas. However they had accomplished it, she applauded their ingenuity and hoped it remained shadowy and unchanged.

Stunned by all she had seen, she reluctantly pulled away from the window wondering what it would take to live in such a place.

"If you don't mind me asking, how much do you pull down a year?"

"Pull down?" he quizzed.

"Money, what's your salary?" she clarified.

"Ohhh, that. Christmas Industries is a non-profit. We don't make any money or use it here."

"Get out of here!" she exclaimed. "You mean everything is free."

"Yep."

"I need to move here and quit paying bills," she murmured under her breath.

Making her way into his secretary's office, she felt a sudden urgency descending.

"Is this your secretary, Claire?" she guessed after seeing the framed family portrait standing behind a clear glass nameplate.

"I think so," he shouted from his office.

Beverley took a seat behind Claire's desk and began taking stock of the contents for anything that would aid in their quest.

"Why don't you give her a call," she suggested as he wandered in.

Christmas Present stared blankly at Beverley.

"You don't remember the number," she stated matter-of-factly. Strangely enough, she had overcome her frustration in dealing with his memory shortfall. His pleasant demeanor and exuberant innocence made those around him want to care and act as surrogates supplying the little extras they, and more importantly he, knew were missing but never allowed to get in the way of whatever task he was assigned. He was the living embodiment of the ethereal sentiment that kept humanity yearning for a better tomorrow . . . hope.

"Okay, let's see," said Beverley scouting Claire's desk. "There has to be something here that can help us."

Claire's desk was a tribute to secretaries everywhere. Her files were immaculately arranged and filed, notes legibly written and complete, even her 'junk' drawer, filled with office supplies and an inordinate stockpile of index cards and post-it notes of every color, was arranged in an orderly fashion. The only thing that could have been considered out of place was the bobble headed Santa that shouted 'Ho, Ho, Ho,' when rocked. Nothing however, pointed to any information about Arthur or Austen.

While reaching for the appointment book, Beverley inadvertently bumped the computer mouse, causing the screen to 'wake-up'. The last screenshot Claire had viewed contained Arthur's information and immediately popped up.

"Hey, look!" exclaimed Beverley excitedly, "Arthur's file is on screen!"

Christmas Present quickly stepped around the desk and leaned in over Beverley's shoulder to view the information as she pointed it out with the cursor.

"Birthday, birthplace, family info, childhood pictures, letters to Santa, naughty and nice ratings; wow, is there anything you guys don't know about us?" she asked no one in particular.

"Apparently not," responded Christmas Present.

Beverley felt a little guilty looking at Arthur's personal information and resisted the urge to read his childhood letters to Santa, but could not help panning through his pictures. She smiled at images of him dressed in ridiculously cute outfits mothers sometimes dress young boys in, then laughed out loud at a picture of him sitting in a high chair holding aloft a wooden spoon filled with what appeared to be cake icing. His toothless grin pasted on a chubby face smeared with the chocolate confection was so precious she wanted to e-mail it to herself and have it blown up so she could surprise him with it on his birthday.

She continued to select a few links until she saw one labeled 'find'.

"Here we go. 'Find'. Maybe this will tell us where he is."

After selecting the link, the program, 'Google Earth', launched. The earth slowly rotated and tilted on the screen until the North Pole dominated the frame. The image continued to zoom in closer and closer until a 'currently located at' marker planted itself firmly in the midst of the city.

"He's here!" Beverley cried out. "Arthur's here!"

"Where? What's the address?"

"I don't know, hold on a second." Beverley clicked on the marker. "2520 Winter Wonderland Parkway. Where's that?"

Christmas Present shrugged unawareness.

"Never mind. See if you can find a street map or directory," she ordered.

Christmas Present began his search as Beverley grabbed a stationary pad to scribble down the address. Halfway through her note taking she noticed the tiny address printed on the bottom of the pad. *'Christmas Industries, 2525 Winter Wonderland Parkway'*.

"Christmas Present? What's the name of the building across the street?"

"That's the Gift Wrapping complex," he answered after looking out the window.

"According to this, Arthur is somewhere in there."

"What's he doing over there?" Christmas Present wondered aloud.

"I don't know, but that where we're headed as soon as I check on Austen."

Filled with a sense of accomplishment, Beverley rapidly typed in Austen's name and clicked 'find'. A graphic of the earth slowly spun as she impatiently watched, *c'mon, c'mon, hurry up,* waiting for it to stop and indicate success. After a few minutes, the search box flashed 'No Location Found', leaving Beverley deflated and baffled at the outcome. *Where are you Austen? Maybe Arthur will know something when we find him.*

CHAPTER 29

Santa's sleigh hovered above the rooftop of the Fisher duplex. While his tiny associates went about meeting their prearranged engagements, Santa unbuckled Austen and hoisted her into his arms.

"You ready sweetheart."

Austen nodded, wrapped her arms around his neck and placed her head on his shoulder.

This was a delicate situation for Santa. He needed to reunite Austen with Arthur. She had been through a terrible ordeal and understandably would want to see her father, but that would not be possible right now. What he knew, but she did not, was that Arthur was on a scheduled visit with Christmas Present and there was a possibility that both were in the home at that very moment. Christmas Present usually started his presentation there before taking his client on short field trips to look in on others less fortunate to reinforce his message of charity, and then returned to the home before Christmas Future's scheduled arrival at one o'clock.

He needed to get in, put Austen to bed, work his magic to induce sleep and in the morning both she and Arthur would awaken with one heck of a story to tell each other about the dreams both had had the night before.

"Carlton, don't worry about me. Keep delivering the gifts on schedule," he instructed. "I'll be back soon."

"Yes, sir."

Moments later, Santa and Austen faded from view and reappeared in her bedroom. Santa motioned her to be quiet and gently set her down on the edge of the bed. The instant he released his grip, she darted from the room.

"Austen!" he bellowed in a hushed tone. "Come back here!" By the time he entered the hallway she was entering Arthur's bedroom.

"Daddy? Daddy? Where are you?"

He closed in quietly, prepared to disappear from view at any moment. Suddenly, she emerged from the empty bedroom and flew by him heading towards the stairs steadily screaming for Arthur.

Santa ran after her, surprised that someone so small could move so quickly and then thought of his delivery elves. By the time he caught up with her, she had already made the rounds of the entire downstairs and stood crying in the kitchen.

"My daddy's gone! Christmas Past took him," she screamed.

Most parents were used to seeing their children crying, but for Santa, the sight of tears on the face of someone so young was enough to break his heart. He stooped and hugged Austen to his chest, stroking her hair gently as he whispered, "Shhhhh. It's okay sweetheart. We're going to find your dad."

His reassurance was enough to quiet her for the moment. He assumed that Christmas Present had probably taken Arthur out on location, but somewhere deep inside he felt the gnaw of danger eating at him. Nothing had gone right this night so far.

There was no doubt in his mind that Christmas Present played no part in the plot, whatever it was. Knowing the temperament of Christmas Past and the liabilities of Christmas Present, there was no way she could trust him with anything complicated. Her patience, already razor thin, could barely deal with him on a daily basis. The thought of her constantly having to keep him updated on the minute details necessary to accomplish anything on this scale was ridiculous.

Maybe Austen had left something out in the relaying of her story. Some tiny fact she thought unimportant that may provide the key to unlocking the widening mystery. Adults under stress often left out facts they thought insignificant, but in the end provided investigators with the vital clue needed to solve a case. Children's memories were as delicate and sporadic as their actions and required constant cajoling to unlock any hidden thoughts.

"Why would she take your dad?" asked Santa.

"I don't know, but she did. I know she did," argued Austen.

Lest she dart off again, he picked her up and placed her on his knee as he took a seat at the island. He had no real basis to believe or grant merit to her accusation. But then again, he would never have thought it possible for a child to pop up in the North Pole, then escape and stowaway on his sleigh. Based on those set of facts, he placed much weight on her argument.

"I'm sure he's around here somewhere. Let's look together, but let me go first. Trust me, I'm pretty good at sneaking around people's homes."

Holding Austen in his arms, Santa searched the bottom of the house. He was looking less for Arthur than he was looking for any sign that Christmas Present was there. After working with the ghost for nearly two centuries, he could usually 'feel' the ghost's presence.

"I told you Christmas Past took my daddy!" declared Austen as tears began to well in her eyes.

"Now hold on sweetheart. We don't know that," said Santa trying to appease the child and raise her spirits. "Maybe he stepped out for a little bit."

"Nooooo, he would never do that," she argued. "He would never go anywhere or let me go anywhere . . . Ms. Beverley!" realized Austen suddenly. "He might be next door at Ms. Beverley's house!"

"Okay, okay, shhhh," said Santa in a hushed voice to reassure her. "Let's go and see."

Afraid to put Austen down lest she take off and wake up the neighborhood, Santa decided upon another course of action. He proceeded into the foyer and stood on the staircase landing against the inner wall separating the two units.

"Before we go rip roaring around Ms. Beverley's home in the middle of the night, I think it best I should make sure the coast is, ahem, clear, shall we say," he said with a wink.

"Okay," replied Austen.

What he did not want to say was that the last thing he needed her to see was her father and Beverley in a compromising position in front of a cozy fireplace. He had run into such scenes many times in the past and knew that a certain amount of discretion was necessary.

Austen watched in amazement as he stuck his head through the wall. From his vantage point, he could see into the living room and partially into the kitchen, but not as far as the backroom or anywhere upstairs. He listened intently with hypersensitive ears for any sounds of lovemaking, but only heard an intermittent crackle from the dying fire beneath Christmas music. The home appeared empty. He sighed knowing his assessment would never satisfy Austen's curiosity.

"The coast looks clear to me. Let's go over and take a closer look." Before Austen had a chance to respond, both were standing in Beverley's foyer. He set Austen on her feet and like the winner of a shopping spree with sixty seconds to grab anything in the store for free, she tore through the home looking for any sign of life as Santa waited.

"She's gone! Christmas Past took Beverley too! We gotta find them!" screeched Austen upon her return.

"And we will Austen, we will. I have a few more deliveries to make. After that, we'll hurry back to the North Pole and find your daddy and Beverley. Okay?"

"But what if she tries to hurt them like she did the doctor?"

Santa kneeled and held her close. "If they're at the North Pole, no one there is going to hurt them. They'll be fine."

"You promise?" she insisted.

"Cross my heart and hope to die."

CHAPTER 30

Four brawny security elves followed the Ghost of Christmas Past wearing scowls that matched her own. They bracketed an optimistic looking Arthur as the procession made its way through the maze of dimly lit corridors.

Their lengthy trek ended at yet another door through which they stepped onto a snowy courtyard bordered by a high wall partially covered with ivy. Under the impression that his reunification with Austen was imminent, Arthur barely took notice of the candy cane striped pole erected a few paces in front of the wall. Christmas Past held back and silently watched as Arthur, led by one elf and trailed by another, dutifully kept pace until they stopped beside the pole. Confusion registered on his face as they executed an about face, grabbed him by each arm, backed him against the pole and began to bind his hands and ankles.

Arthur looked into the eyes of Christmas Past for an explanation.

"Why am I being tied up again? You said I could see Austen, and we could leave together."

"I did, didn't I," she sighed. "But that was before I learned our security forces were looking for a dangerous intruder matching your description."

"An intruder?"

Christmas Past's coy smile provided the first hint of fraud.

"Who . . . me? But you brought me here!" he protested.

"That's right, I did," she agreed. "To interrogate you. And after hours of questioning, I finally uncovered your heinous plot."

"What plot?" he questioned with exasperation.

"The one you've been patiently planning for years and waiting until your daughter was old enough to help execute. After all, you couldn't trust anyone else to help you assassinate Santa Claus!"

Her cavalier tone unnerved him. He suddenly realized that everything that had happened so far was part of a grand scheme she had planned for some time. Though he did not know the full details, he knew that he and Austen were unwitting pawns in her sweeping conspiracy. But to what end?

"WHAT! That's crazy!" he shouted.

"I agree. You'd have to be crazy to poison a child's mind with so many lies about Santa that she would help you smuggle a bomb on board his sleigh."

If the allegation stunned him, the implication was devastating.

"Where's Austen? You said she was here!"

"She was until she cleverly escaped from her confines and stowed away on Santa's sleigh. I have to commend you on your planning and execution of this crime, Mr. Fisher. It was most impressive." Her feigned pride was smug and complete.

A veil of desperation began to descend around Arthur. His mind was overwhelmed with activity and stifled by his inability to get beyond the growing clutter she was feeding him, choking out any possibility of figuring out what to do next to extract himself from his predicament. It was as if he were stuck in quicksand, slowly sinking. Any move he made to free himself only resulted in him sinking farther into the sandy abyss. The fetters binding his hands and feet sapped whatever strength he had left to fight and negated any notion of escape or rescue.

"I haven't committed any crime," he said flatly.

All heads turned as Sebastian darted into the courtyard carrying a leather case and wearing a satisfied grin.

"I would never have imagined such a thing was even possible, Mr. Fisher, had you not confessed to it!" roared Christmas Past.

Sebastian opened the case and took out a portable media player. He flipped open the screen and presented it to Christmas Past. She in turn walked it over to Arthur, held it close enough for him to view and pressed 'play'. The use of multiple cameras and harsh overhead lighting to film his impromptu interrogation cast his eyes in shadow and removed any semblance of humility from his face. The grainy texture, jump cuts, extreme close-ups, cut aways and menacing sound effects combined to create an on screen monster worthy of destruction.

"What is your name?" asked the over-dubbed voice of Christmas Past.

"*Arthur Fisher,*" he responded in a mechanically altered voice to sound hollow and distinctly unapologetic.

"*You couldn't have pulled off a crime of this magnitude without an accomplice. Who else was involved in this conspiracy to kill Santa?*"

"*My daughter, Austen.*"

"*You are an unspeakably evil man to involve a child in something like this! Surely there must be some regret on your part. How do you feel knowing that you are responsible for the death of Santa?*"

"*Like a child on Christmas morning!*"

That response, shown with him happily prancing about the lab was devastating.

"*This is absurd! What do you think the peaceful and generous inhabitants of the North Pole are going to say when they learn you killed our precious leader?*"

"*I really don't care --*"

"*Why did you hate him so much? What did you have against a sainted figure that dedicated his entire existence to bringing happiness to the children of the world?*"

"*. . . he was a fat, selfish jerk who deserves to die --*"

With that final acknowledgement, she shut the media player off.

"You manipulated my words and set me up!" Arthur objected angrily. "You're trying to frame me! I am not saying another word! I want a lawyer!"

His vacuous demand caused Christmas Past and Sebastian to break out in a fit of laughter.

"You don't need a lawyer. Lawyers are for trials, Mr. Fisher," managed Christmas Past, still amused by his plight. "You're not going on trial."

"I'm not?"

"No, you idiot! How can you go on trial when you were shot and killed trying to escape?" howled the Ghost of Christmas Past.

Even the strapping stoic faced security elves lowered their impassive masks and joined in the laughter, leaving Arthur to shut his eyes and contemplate why of all the nights in the year tragedy would choose Christmas Eve to visit him.

❄ ❄ ❄ ❄ ❄ ❄ ❄

Beverley, followed by Christmas Present, trudged through the snow toward the entrance of the Gift Wrapping Facility.

"Are you sure this is it?" he asked.

"Yep," confirmed Beverley pointing out the address in large type above the entrance. "2520 Winter Wonderland Parkway."

Though locked, Christmas Present tugged at the door's handles anyway.

"What do we do now?"

"How should I know, you work and live here," replied Beverley. Increasingly, their roles were shifting to the point that Christmas Present was relying more on her judgment than she on his.

"Wait a minute, you're a ghost. Can't you just walk through the door and unlock it?" she rationalized.

"I suppose I could," assumed Present.

Something inside Beverley told her it was going to happen. If history was any indication, it had to. Christmas Present composed himself, closed his eyes and strode confidently into the door. As Beverley feared, he hit the door with such force he fell backwards, nearly knocked unconscious by the thick pane.

The initial shock concerned Beverley, but when she saw that he was okay, the urge to laugh at yet another faux pas on his part bubbled to the surface.

"I guess not," she mused helping him to his feet and brushing snow from his jacket. She stepped back and inspected the exterior of the building "There has to be another way in. Any thoughts?"

"Maybe I can transport us inside," he suggested.

"Whoa! Before we do that, let's try and locate another entrance," she advised. "Arthur, and maybe Austen are inside this building. I don't want to end up on the other side of town or some swamp in Florida."

She grabbed Christmas Present's arm and pulled him along. "C'mon, maybe there's a loading dock or some other way in around back."

Arthur watched helplessly as Sebastian stowed the media player and handed Christmas Past an ornate wooden box.

"Thank you, Sebastian."

She measured a few paces away from Arthur, knelt, placed the box on the ground, and then pulled out a gold chain from around her neck previously hidden underneath her blouse.

Hanging from it were a small silver key and a larger, paddle shaped handle.

"You know what the biggest perk of living and working in the North Pole is, Mr. Fisher?"

"The weather?"

"Now that's comedy! Even in the face of death, you maintain a sense of humor. Good for you," she mocked.

"No, not the weather . . . it's the toys!" she gleefully extolled. "You wouldn't think it to look at me, but I absolutely *love* toys, especially, what do you humans call them . . . the 'old school' ones."

She unlocked the box and lifted out a small velvet bag tied with a ribbon. She methodically untied the knot as if savoring the moment and gently pulled out a mechanical soldier resembling an eighteenth century Nutcracker.

"These are my favorite. They are *soooooo* beautiful," she said running her laced fingers over the toys' gilded exterior. "Look at the hand crafting and ornate detail . . . absolutely exquisite! You can't buy these at Wal-Mart!"

She slowly turned the soldier over and wound it with the larger paddle shaped handle on the chain. After doing so, she cleared a spot in the snow and gently placed him on the ground. All eyes watched as he began to whir, shouldered his tiny rifle, stiffly marched a few paces, stopped, then executed a sharp turn to face Arthur before snapping to a 'parade rest' position.

"Omigod! He is so cute!" clapped Christmas Past while screeching with delight at the little performance. Arthur shook his head in disbelief at her display of madness as she raced to set up the remaining soldiers. When finished, a line of eight tiny soldiers stood facing him.

"You can't be serious. You're going to order tin soldiers to execute me?" he joked half-heartedly.

"Of course not. Quit being stupid!" she rebuked. She reached inside the box and removed the remaining bag. Slightly larger than the others, she untied the top revealing a general wielding a sword and held it up for Arthur to see. "He's giving the order," she stated politely.

By now, Arthur had reached a point of equilibrium. He had given up any hope of rescue or release from his waking nightmare and like many a condemned man, accepted his fate. The surreal nature of his imminent demise only added to his acceptance. It was almost comic. In this place, the line between reality and fantasy intertwined, weaving a tapestry of implausibility so complex that, like Ebenezer Scrooge, he could no longer trust his senses and therefore decided to abandon them for the sake of his mental well being.

He would play his part in this elaborately constructed morality tale and wake up in the morning with one hell of a hangover and wonderful tale to tell Austen and Beverley. The unseen benefit to this dark cloud was that he would probably put pen to paper and write about his experience with so much authenticity that he would become the next great fiction novelist. If he were lucky, perhaps Hollywood would come calling and turn his tale into a blockbuster movie.

Sebastian approached and held out a blindfold. Arthur rejected his offer with a shake of his head thinking that if he were to write about this, he needed to see and remember as much as possible.

"Very well," replied Sebastian and retreated to a position alongside Christmas Past.

"Do you have any last words?" she asked winding up the tiny general.

"Yeah. I can't wait until I wake up tomorrow morning so I can tell Austen about this dream. I just hope I remember everything."

"Good luck with that . . . only one of us will," she replied glibly, then placed the general on the ground and backed away. "You know what they say about dying in your own dream."

Arthur smiled as the tiny General marched into position and with a raspy mechanical voice, exclaimed, "To the ready!"

The line of toy soldiers followed his orders with precision and snapped to attention.

He raised his tiny sword and commanded, "Take your aim . . . aim . . . aim . . . " The general's sword jerked in rhythm to his jammed repetition. Christmas Past tromped forward, picked up the toy and inspected it. Suddenly, a thought crossed her face. She spun on her heels looking around the courtyard with an evil eye.

"Christmas Present? I know you're there. Come out from your hiding place!"

The team of security elves panned out along with Sebastian, scouring the shadows for any sign of movement.

"If you don't come out, I will give the order to fire myself. Your silly little parlor tricks have no effect on me!" she threatened.

From a dark corner to the rear of the courtyard farthest from Arthur, Christmas Present and Beverley slowly emerged.

"Beverley!" cried Arthur.

Before she could respond, the team of security elves raced forward and surrounded them, then pushed them forward to face the wrath of the Ghost of Christmas Past.

CHAPTER 31

Less than a mile away from the drama unfolding in the courtyard, the local broadcast anchors, Cole Winter and Holly Bush, shouted over the real and artificially amplified crowd noise.

"Santa should be wrapping up his deliveries in a matter of moments and returning to the North Pole. And you know what that means, don't you Holly?" he asked, mindful to smile broadly and keep a three-quarter profile for the camera.

"I sure do Cole," she answered with an equally insincere perkiness, "Touchdown!"

The raucous crowds of partygoers gathered below them began to chant 'Touchdown' while tossing hats and cushions in the air.

"And this year's touchdown fireworks show promises to be the biggest ever, Cole!"

"We'll see, Holly. Planners say it will be so spectacular that it may even dim the unusually bright northern light show we've been seeing since we've been on the air."

While they continued to babble, filling airtime with mundane observations, the large screen in the square flashed a graphic of the globe showing Santa's progress and estimated time of arrival. Each minute that came off the clock sent the crowd into yet another frenzied cheer.

❄ ❄ ❄ ❄ ❄ ❄ ❄

"You want to explain what's going on here?" demanded Christmas Present.

"Gladly. Justice is being served. Mr. Fisher, along with his daughter, has been found guilty of a criminal conspiracy to kill Santa Claus!" Christmas Past announced with authority.

Christmas Present's eyes grew wide at the shocking revelation. "No!" he voiced with astonishment.

"Don't believe her, Present. It's a lie!" said Beverley stepping forward to confront the charge and defend Arthur. "Arthur wouldn't hurt anyone!"

"Then why did he confess?" asked Christmas Past calmly.

"He confessed?" Beverley and Christmas Present looked at each other with both shock and confusion. She could not believe what she was hearing and turned to Arthur for clarification.

"Arthur . . . what's she saying?"

"She's just trying to frame me and Austen, that's all. You know I would never do anything like that. I don't even believe in Santa Claus!"

Everyone, with the exception of Beverley, gasped in horror and stared at Arthur with contempt. Even the tiny soldiers furrowed their tin eyebrows and shook their metal heads in disapproval.

No one seemed more offended than Christmas Present. "You may get away with that in your world, Mr. Fisher, but denial of Santa's existence is a serious crime here in the North Pole!" he stated authoritatively, then turned to Beverley and added. "Even I remember that."

Realizing his blunder, Arthur quickly withdrew his statement. "Okay, okay, I'm sorry, he's real. But ask yourself, why would I try to kill him? What's my motive?"

"Your lack of Christmas spirit!" countered Christmas Past. "That's why Christmas Present requested that I and Christmas Future visit you in the first place. Isn't that right?"

"That is correct," he concurred. "Christmas Past is right about that."

Beverley looked on wide-eyed. The whole affair was taking on a courtroom feel and had it been an official trial, based on the circumstantial evidence presented so far, she was afraid that an elfin jury would have voted to convict Arthur. Yet, having a lackadaisical attitude toward Christmas was hardly a reason to execute someone.

"I'm right about this conspiracy as well," stated Christmas Past in her best prosecutorial tenor. "But in the interest of fairness and considering a human life hangs in the balance, I'll allow you to review the evidence. Unlike Mr. Fisher, it does not lie!"

"Fair enough," agreed Christmas Present.

"Sebastian, take Christmas Present and show him the taped interrogation in its entirety."

"Yes ma'am."

Christmas Present turned to Beverley, "Stay here, I'll be back in a little while. And don't worry everything will be alright, I promise."

"Okay," said Beverley.

The moment they disappeared through the courtyard door, Christmas Past focused her eyes on Beverley.

"I don't believe you've had the pleasure. I am the Ghost -- "

"Of Christmas Past," spat Beverley. "I know who you are! Why are you doing this? What's this really all about?"

"She's planning to release some kind of spray that forces humans to have Christmas spirit," shouted Arthur.

"People already have lots of Christmas spirit. Why would you do something like that?"

"For the money. What else is there?" shrugged Christmas Past.

"You going to ruin Christmas over money?"

The question seemed to strike a dissonant chord in Christmas Past. Her bemused expression morphed into a scowl of resentment that displayed the depth of poisoned memories that had been collecting for decades.

"In case you haven't noticed, Christmas is already ruined. It used to be defined by what you 'gave', now it's all about what 'I got'. Christmas is supposed to be a peaceful time to reflect upon the less fortunate amongst you. A holiday that bridges the gap of wealth and social status, a time to surrender to the better parts of your nature and give of yourself and share with friends and strangers alike."

"It used to be the most special time of the year, now it's the most loathsome and all you humans do is whine about how you can't wait until it's over. What started as twelve wonderful days of gaiety has turned into a 'Holiday Season' that lasts for three months. No wonder you've grown tired of it. Christmas decorations are in stores before Halloween candy. Fewer and fewer children believe in Santa or even know what he stands for!"

"You think Christmas tradition started with, 'A Christmas Carol'? Who do you think gave ole Charlie Dickens the idea for his story? We did! It started with us! It wasn't meant to be a fictional tale; it was a manual informing you ponderous peasants of the error of your selfish ways - an invitation to participate in the wondrous possibilities Christmas had to offer."

"Our only purpose here is to serve mankind by trying to bring some lasting joy into your world. But somewhere along the way your wretched souls have grown dark with greed and are no longer filled with good will towards your fellow man. And since you no longer appreciate our gift, I'll follow your lead and do what humans do the day after Christmas with gifts they don't want. I'll simply return it and get my MONEY BACK!"

Beverley could do little but accept Christmas Past's outburst. Her appraisal of humanity's inadequacies was dead on. There was little to defend; yet, Beverley stood on the tenet that it was wrong to condemn the entirety of mankind for the failings of a few.

A few? No, Christmas Past was right, it was more than a few. Statistically, it was nearly all. Unless you were a child, the anxiety over the coming holiday held no real joy. Children's gifts, especially the much-desired electronic ones, were so expensive that many families went into debt to appease their children's desires. Companies staked their financial futures on holiday sales and left no stone unturned to reach potential buyers under the marketed guise of Christmas spirit. The more money you spent, the more Christmas spirit you had. It was no wonder the holidays left humans jaded and primary amongst them was Arthur. Still, Christmas Past had no right to take his life and plot to ruin everyone else's.

"You're right, I agree. Mankind has lost its way. Some of us are greedy and petty and only care about material possessions. We have allowed corporations to over commercialize the holidays and turn them into shopping sprees. But, we can change," pleaded Beverley.

"Change. Why would I want you to change when I can profit from it?" countered Christmas Past. "If mankind needs a little Christmas spirit, who am I to deny them? Here it is."

She reached into her pocket and produced the bottle of fragrance waving it for Beverley to see.

"You think Christmas starts earlier and earlier each year. Wait until next year. It's never going to end. One whiff of this concoction and *every day* will be Christmas. From what Dr. Hamilton tells me –"

"Dr. Hamilton? Dr. Charles Hamilton?" questioned Beverley.

"Yes, familiar with him are you? According to our able chemist, the scent is quite addictive. This," she proudly exclaimed shaking the bottle, "represents years of research and millions of dollars in investment."

"Christmas Present said you don't use money here. Where'd you get it? Did you steal it?"

"Quite literally, yes. I wait until your various state lotteries grow large enough to matter and someone wins. Then I go back and buy a winning ticket for the previous week. Wish you'd though of that, huh?"

"With this potent elixir, everything changes. It will cause humans to become more of what they already are, mindless consumers. You will work from sunrise to sunrise like zombies to buy more than what you can afford, because after all, what is Christmas without gifts."

"With Santa out of the way and yours truly at the helm, Christmas Industries will no longer be a non-profit entity. We have the technology to manufacture and distribute more goods in a week than China, Mexico and India in a year! We will enter your capitalistic marketplace, go public and become bigger than the top ten companies on the Fortune 500, combined! And 'you know who' will be the majority stockholder. If you're nice, sweetheart," she said stroking Beverley's cheek, "I might just let you in on the initial public offering."

"That's a stupid plan. It will never work," said Beverley with disgust.

"You don't think so. Ask your friend; he's sampled the goods." She held the fragrance aloft for Arthur to see, waving it like a hypnotist inducing a patient. "Would you like another whiff, Mr. Fisher?"

Arthur's eyes fixated on the bottle, following its every move like a cat watching a bouncing ball just out of reach. Beverley could see the truth of Christmas Past's claim on Arthur's face and felt her spirit fade.

"I know that look. It's despair," summarized Christmas Past. "The point when reality leaves nothing to the imagination and all hope is abandoned."

Angered by Christmas Past's suffocating smugness, Beverley mounted a look of defiance intended to relay that regardless of the circumstance, she still had hope. Christmas Past, however, saw through her courageous façade with an ease that comes with centuries of wisdom.

"I know what you're thinking. This is the point in the movie where the evil genius, after detailing her plan to the sympathetic hero, gets what's coming and meets her deserved end. Unfortunately my dear, this isn't a movie." Christmas Past leaned in close, extending her finger for emphasis. "I can assure you with absolute certainty, my sweet, Mr. Fisher *will* die in a matter of moments, as will Santa and by extension, Austen. As for you and the gracious Dr. Hamilton, you will be returned to your past where neither will be the wiser."

The inevitability of her words brought tears to Beverley's eyes. "No, you're wrong. You're wrong!" she cried. "Christmas Present won't let that happen!"

"Christmas Present?" laughed Past. "Is that who you're relying on to save you?"

❄ ❄ ❄ ❄ ❄ ❄ ❄

Santa's sleigh hovered idly above the remote reaches of a scientific outpost on Antarctica (coincidentally, it was not far from where Christmas Present and Beverley initially appeared). The last gift delivered, the crew congratulated themselves on a job well done.

'Roto' Richie, the reigning delivery champion sat dejected. He held his head in his hands wondering how it was he had the misfortune of pulling the assignment containing Austen's package. The loss of delivery time had resulted in his falling two gifts short of retaining his crown.

Watching as the elves had made their rounds, Austen had learned of the competition and become aware of his dilemma. Throughout the night, she had acted as his personal cheerleader, and now, knowing he fell short because of her made her feel terrible.

"I'm sorry I made you lose," she apologized.

She was the first human child he had ever met. Her sadness was palpable and made him feel like a heel. It was his job to make children like her smile. His five-year winning streak spoke to the fact that no one else was better at doing that than he.

Richie was aware of her quandary. Here it was, Christmas, and she faced the uncertainty of reuniting with her father. He had two children of his own awaiting his return and the thought of them ever being subjected to her predicament was too much for him to stomach.

"That's okay, Austen, there are more important things than a silly award." He smiled and tussled her hair and she responded by giving him a hug followed by a kiss on the cheek.

"Well done, crew," praised Santa. "Now let's point this sleigh northward and get home to our families so we can celebrate and enjoy our Christmas."

The crew sent up a cheer as Santa led Austen toward the cockpit.

"Are we going to find my daddy and Beverley now?" she asked.

"They're the last two names on my list."

He lifted her into her seat and buckled her harness, then set the final switch positions on his control panel for the speedy trip home.

"I'll let you do the honors. See that mode switch right there?" he said pointing to a toggle switch within reach of her short arms.

"Yes."

"It's on 'delivery' mode right now. Switch it to 'cruise' and we'll be on our way home."

"Okay."

Austen carefully flipped the switch and listened as the sleigh's motor emitted a high-pitched whine. Moments before the sleigh shot into the night, the solid red light on the ominous black box attached to the undercarriage began to flash rapidly.

CHAPTER 32

Sebastian followed a meandering route through the maze of corridors with Christmas Present in tow. Unsure of their eventual destination, Christmas Present tapped the diminutive point man on his shoulder.

"Excuse me, what was your name again?" he asked.

"Sebastian, sir."

"Sebastian, weren't you supposed to be showing me something?"

"Yes, sir. You were on your way to see the fireworks display and somehow you got turned around down here. It happens all the time. You asked me to show you the quickest way out," replied Sebastian without the slightest hint of sarcasm.

"The fireworks display," recognized Present. "That's right, Santa should be returning any minute now. I almost forgot!"

"That's okay, sir," smiled Sebastian deceptively. "Keep following this corridor and take the first door you see. It leads to the main floor. Follow the red line to the sleigh pad. You should have an excellent view from there."

"Straight ahead, take the first door and . . ."

"Follow the red line."

"Follow the red line. Got it. Thank you!"

"Anytime, sir. Glad to be of assistance."

Christmas Present turned to leave, but Sebastian stopped him, "Oh, one more thing, sir."

"What's that?"

Making Christmas Present the butt of his joke wasn't enough for the vindictive elf; he needed to deliver a punch line that would bring the house down later on.

"Merry Christmas, sir!"

"Merry Christmas to you too . . ."

"Sebastian, sir."

"Merry Christmas, Sebastian!"

Sebastian waved goodbye and followed Christmas Present with his eyes until he disappeared from view. He waited and listened for the echo of the door opening and closing to indicate the absent-minded spirit had executed his bogus instructions to a tee.

"What an idiot," snickered Sebastian. Satisfied that Christmas Present was out of the picture for good, Sebastian sprinted through a series of shortcuts and emerged grinning in the courtyard.

"Where's Christmas Present?" asked Beverley anxiously.

"You mean, Christmas Preoccupied. He's on his way to watch Santa light up the sky."

Christmas Past and Sebastian shared a hearty laugh and why not? They had won. But ever the student of history, Christmas Past could recall every battle and eventual war lost by overconfident commanders who reveled in their bright future, only to mismanage the present and eventually become a scourge of the past. There was still a certain matter needing her attention before any real celebration could begin. She checked her watch. *No time like the present.*

"Shall we get on with this?" asked Christmas Past.

Beverley had reached the lowest point imaginable. With Austen and Santa speeding towards their doom, Arthur trussed up awaiting execution and no discernible hope of salvation by Christmas Present, she buried her head in her hands and began to cry.

"Heyyyyy, stop that," soothed Arthur. "Everything is going to work out fine."

"No it's not," cried Beverley. Sensing this may be her first and last opportunity to hold him, she sprinted across the icy courtyard and hugged him tightly, burying her head in the nape of his neck as her tears flowed openly.

Had he been granted one wish, Arthur would have asked to at least have his hands untied so he could hold her. The sounds of her sobbing brought tears to his eyes, though he fought to remain strong for her sake.

"Remember the dream I had and I said it seemed so real?" he reminisced. "This is just a part of it."

Beverley raised her head and wiped her eyes. She forced a smile at the sight of his tears and gently wiped them from his face. "It doesn't feel like a dream," she whimpered.

"That's because it's my dream and you're in it." He closed his eyes as if reliving a memory. "Right now, I'm sitting next to you in front of your fireplace. It's so cozy and warm I dozed off and as soon as I wake up, I'll tell you everything that happened."

"You promise."

He opened his eyes and stared deep into hers. "I promise. And since this is my dream, I can embarrass myself and tell you anything, even . . . that I love you."

His confession hit her hard. Her tears flowed freely through her smile and gave Arthur the response she didn't have the strength to voice.

"Don't worry, I'll leave that part out."

"You better not," she said and kissed him hard.

"Awhhhh, how sweet," mocked Christmas Past.

Sebastian approached and once again offered Arthur a blindfold. He shook off the offer and continued to stare in Beverley's tear-filled eyes as Sebastian pocketed the fabric and separated the two lovers.

"Any last words, Mr. Fisher?" asked Christmas Past.

Ignoring her, Arthur directed his last statement towards Beverley as Sebastian guided her away. "When I wake up, I'll go check on Austen and bring back more egg nog."

"And I'll supply the rum."

With everyone standing at a safe distance, Christmas Past set the tiny general on the ground. As before, he stepped through his mechanical routine and addressed his troops.

"To the ready!"

Arthur smiled at Beverley, who in turn silently mouthed, 'I love you.'

As the distant crowds countdown neared zero, Arthur turned his gaze to the wonder of the heavens displaying the shimmering Northern lights waving like neon curtains preparing to close after the final act. What appeared to be a shooting star blazed across the sky moments after he closed his eyes and issued a silent prayer for Austen.

"Aim . . ."

Quietly sobbing, Beverley clasped her hands and closed her eyes tightly while repeating, "Remember Arthur and Austen. Remember Arthur and Austen. Remember Arthur and Austen."

"FIRE!"

An immense flash of light marked the appearance of the sleigh above the sleigh pad. Simultaneously, the report of the soldiers' rifles mingled with the sight and sounds of fireworks accompanying a large explosion that sent an astonishing display skyward to the roar and delight of the crowd, completely unaware that a double tragedy had just taken place.

COLIN QUASHIE

THE FUTURE

"*Are these the shadows of the things that Will be, or are they shadows of things that May be, only? Men's courses will foreshadow certain ends, to which, if persevered in, they must lead. But if the courses be departed from, the ends will change. Say it is thus with what you show me!*"

- **A Christmas Carol**, Charles Dickens

CHAPTER 33

Beverley wearily opened her eyes. She looked around as if awakened from a deep sleep holding the clipboard containing the passenger manifest. She stared at it wistfully, trying to remember why she was even interested in the list of names.

She sighed, closed her eyes and massaged them with her thumb and middle finger. *Some flights are just too damn long,* and this one had just begun. Mentally drained, she wished she had the power to speed up time. The three-week Christmas vacation awaiting her could not get there fast enough.

She had no elaborate plans and would take the time to relax and enjoy the season without the usual rush. During her first week, she would buy a tree, decorate her apartment and go Christmas shopping. She normally worked over the holidays, trying to save enough money to buy a house, but this year she was looking forward to spending Christmas with her parents and would drive south to Daytona Beach on Christmas Eve and surprise them. Her sister Zoe had recently given birth to her second child, and Beverley was anxious to hold the best gift anyone could possibly receive this time of year. After that, she would return home, rent a handful of movies and disappear inside her apartment, content to live out her remaining week like a hermit trapped beneath clean sheets and a heavy down comforter until it was time to resume her flight schedule.

The soothing promise of impending relaxation brought order to her disheveled thoughts and nudged free the reason she held the manifest: Dr. Hamilton. She opened her eyes, flipped through the pages and ran a manicured finger down the listing. There it was.

```
Dr. Charles Hamilton / 6a.
```

His name was as plain as the polish on her nails. To verify her find, she poked her head out from behind the curtain and saw him seated peacefully. The reason she had searched for his name in the first place remained a mystery to her. She sighed aloud just as Penney, the other First Class Flight Attendant, entered the galley.

"Bev? Are you okay?" she asked with concern.

"Huh? Yeah. I'm fine. Just a little déjà-vu is all," replied Beverley with a quick smile to cover her embarrassment.

"Uhm-hmm," Penney replied with skepticism. "Does your déjà-vu have a brother? Hell, I'd even settle for a crazy cousin in the basement at this point." They both shared a muzzled laugh before the 'pong' of a passenger call button interrupted them.

"Seat 6a, that's Dr. Hamilton, I'll get it," said Beverley and quickly made her way to his seat.

"Yes, Doctor, how can I help you?"

"You forgot my Coke? No ice."

"I'm very sorry, sir, I'll be back in a moment."

"That's quite alright, young lady. I'm not going anywhere."

Happy to have placed her paranoia exactly where it belonged; behind her, the remainder of the flight was just what Beverley needed, uneventful. Now seated in the back of a cab staring out the window on her way home, Dr. Hamilton could have been a million miles away, so distant were her thoughts.

As the cab rolled along the freeway, she lazily stared at everything, unable to focus on anything. Mile after mile the billboards, strip malls, traffic lights and parking lots rolled by like credits in a pointless movie. She had the feeling of being glued to a stationary platform while the world, represented by an endlessly moving slideshow of images, flickered on and off around her at random intervals. Since her flight, she felt strangely uncoordinated, as if parts of her were assembled incorrectly and needed adjustment to regain balance, both mentally and physically.

Cut off by another driver, the cabbie's horn snapped Beverley from her stasis. Looking ahead for any other signs of impending doom, she locked eyes with the laughing bobble headed Santa on the dashboard and once again found herself drifting through a mental fog infused with imaginary shapes quickly disappearing in misty trails. The Christmas music crackling through the busted speaker brought her back from the shadowy abyss and invited her to begin sharing in all the holiday season had to offer.

Following her instructions, the cab driver exited the freeway and took surface streets through neighborhoods decorated for Christmas. She marveled at the elaborate displays, but it was the gaudy handiwork of over zealous revelers that made her smile. One yard featured the whole cast of Disney's animated characters united in praise of the New Born King. The image of Shrek and the three wise men standing bodyguard to Joseph while Princess Fiona comforted the Virgin Mary was irreverently humorous. It made a perfect statement about the encroaching influence of the corporate world on the Christmas tradition and how accepting people were becoming to the marketing chaos.

The cab stopped short of Beverley's door. She paid the driver, wished him a Merry Christmas and gave him a generous tip, which extracted a second, more sincere 'Merry Christmas' on his part along with an offer to help with her bags. Though tired, she politely declined and lugged her baggage to the front door where a box of newspapers and a bundle of rubber-banded mail awaited her.

The moment she picked up the mail, the rubber band snapped. The sudden sting caused her to drop the bundle, strewing mail across the doormat. The simple act of bending to pick up the scattered pieces brought back the nagging memory of Dr. Hamilton, along with a quick flash of déjà vu that escaped her as suddenly as the snapping of the rubber band.

The first thing she did upon entering her apartment was to take the battery out of her pager and bury it deep within her pocketbook. She would not be making herself available to cover any flights. After that, she turned on the heat, turned off the phone's ringer, and then made a beeline for the bathroom.

She drew a hot bath, added beads and foam, and then gently slid beneath the hot silky water, which finally gave her the feeling she had been craving since London; warmth. She sat soaking up the heat long after her fingers pruned. After drying off, she put on a comfortable pair of flannel pajamas and thick socks, and then headed for the kitchen.

Though relaxed and ready for bed after the hot bath, she wanted to make sure she would sleep peacefully through the night and well into the morning. She plucked a glass from the cabinet, poured a shot of rum, and then searched every corner of the refrigerator for eggnog before realizing she hadn't purchased any. It had been two years since she had even tasted the creamy holiday quaff, yet the craving was as strong as it was puzzling. She looked at the time on the microwave. *The grocery stores are still open.* Only the thought of having to change clothes made her resist the urge to go out and buy some. Disappointed, she stared at the rum for a few moments, drank the shot and then poured herself a glass of red wine.

Her next destination was the living room. She put on some instrumental Christmas music and started a fire with a grocery store log. As the flame embraced the synthetic fuel and grew higher, she closed the fire screen, retrieved her mail and newspapers, and then lazily plopped down on a comfortable floor pillow to delve into the business of sorting her mail.

She began separating the obvious Christmas cards from bills, statements, solicitations and junk mail flyers, until one flyer from the mall urging parents to bring their children to see Santa caught her attention. She unfolded it, scanned the text, and then focused on the picture. In the foreground, the mall Santa sat on his throne with two children on his lap, but in the background, the slightly blurred image of a woman grabbed Beverley's attention. Standing beside a snowy Christmas tree dripping with ornaments, the woman held the hand of a little girl Beverley assumed was her daughter. Pulling the flyer closer, she searched the faces of both mother and child trying to place them. They did not appear familiar, but somehow their presence seemed out of place and gave her pause to wonder why the photographer had chosen this particular image to feature in the ad.

There it was again. It wasn't an image or even a memory this time, only a thought. Why did she care? She didn't.

She tossed the flyer aside and began sorting the newspapers by date. Leafing through the pages, she glanced at the headlines, pausing only to read a few lines of anything that sounded interesting before moving on to the obituaries, and then the comics. She read her favorites and silently wished the editors would start re-running the mischievous antics of 'Calvin and Hobbes' the way they did the tamer 'Peanuts'. She removed the page containing the word games and crossword puzzle and folded them neatly for future completion.

A small article announcing the sole winner of a Mucho-Millions lottery made her smile with envy. She found the full-paged Christmas ads hawking everything from toys to cars obnoxious and tossed them aside with disdain then leaned back against the couch with her wine glass in hand.

This was unlike her. She was tired, but restless. Her mind wandered like a procrastinator, unable, or better yet, unwilling to settle on anything. The slow melodic pace of the Christmas music, usually a source of calm inspiration, annoyed her, so she turned it off and dug through the couch cushions for the television's remote control.

It was a few minutes before eleven o'clock and the local channels were teasing their upcoming news. She was in no mood to hear about murder, car accidents or miraculous animal rescues. Needing the company of something familiar, she began methodically surfing the channels in search of an old movie, the older the better. If she were lucky, she would happen upon 'Miracle on 34th Street' or 'It's A Wonderful Life', Christmas movies she'd seen a hundred times but couldn't help watching until the end regardless of where she entered the story. She finally stumbled upon the original black and white version of 'A Christmas Carol' at the point where Jacob Marley was nearly completing his 'visit' with Ebenezer Scrooge.

'Hear me, my time is nearly gone!' cried Jacob.

'I will, but don't be hard upon me! Don't be flowery, Jacob. Pray!' begged Scrooge.

"This is no light part of my penance. I am here tonight to warn you, that you have yet a chance and hope of escaping my fate. A chance and hope of my procuring, Ebenezer.'

'You were always a good friend to me. Thank you.'

'You will be haunted, by three Spirits,' warned Jacob.

"Three spirits," whispered Beverley as she stared unblinking at the television as though stuck in a hypnotic trance awaiting instructions from beyond the pixilated screen.

'Is that the chance and hope you mentioned, Jacob?'

'It is. Without their visits you cannot hope to shun the path I tread. Expect the first tomorrow when the bell tolls one.'

Déjà-vu seized her in its embrace yet again. She closed her eyes and clenched her fists while chasing the elusive thought that had haunted her since the first brief reflection in the airplane's galley. It was a shadow on the periphery best seen when looking elsewhere. It was that annoying itch between the ear and throat, the lost melody to lyrics known by heart . . . the name on the tip of the tongue.

She fought to spotlight every instance of remembrance since her flight. Flashes of each shot through her mind's eye like reflections in a broken pane of glass. First, Dr. Hamilton, then the bobble head Santa on the cab ride home, the dropped mail on the porch, the rum, the eggnog, the mall flyer with the mother and child, Scrooge, Jacob Marley, three spirits, three spirits . . . three spirits.

'Look to see me no more; and look that, for your own sake, you remember what has passed between us! Remember!'

"Remember. Remember. Remember," she intoned while rocking back and forth, working loose the rust from her memory. *Remember what?* Suddenly, she stopped. The revelation forced open her eyes and made her jaw drop with shock. "Omigod," she cried out, tears welling in her eyes, "Arthur! Austen! Remember Arthur and Austen!"

She fell back against the couch and searched the air, looking for a place to start. She didn't know which was worse, the battle to remember or the war to organize thoughts fighting each other for placement. Some were so distinct they needed no consideration. Others remained mere shards of information and required shaping if they were to fit within the bigger picture.

A measured buzzer emanating from the television pulled her from her thoughts, as if specifically directing her to pay close attention. Soon afterwards, a crawl line began its slow trek across the bottom of the screen displaying the winning 'Cash 3' and 'Play 4' lottery numbers as Ebenezer Scrooge's clock chimed one in the background. She straightened and stared at each number as though she held the winning tickets in her hand and wanted to make sure the numbers were correct. With the advent of her enlightenment, faculties once dull were now hypersensitive and searching to find meaning in any and everything.

"Are you the spirit, sir, whose coming was foretold to me?" asked Scrooge as the lottery numbers continued to scroll.

"I am."

"Who, and what are you?" demanded Scrooge as the 'Fabulous Five' disappeared, quickly followed by the 'Mucho Millions' results.

"I am the Ghost of Christmas Past."

"Long past."

"No. Your past."

"Christmas Past," whispered Beverly, then voiced with surety, "the lottery!"

She scrambled to her knees and furiously plowed through the pile of newspapers until she located the article about the lottery winner. Scanning the text, she came across the name of the only winner of the 268 million-dollar prize, 'Mrs. Sasha C. Pitt'. There was no picture, yet something about the name seemed all too familiar.

Beverley crawled to the roll top desk in the corner of the living room and snatched a pen from the drawer. Using the back of an envelope, she wrote out the name 'Mrs. Sasha C. Pitt' and stared at it, then began rearranging the letters, crossing them out on the original name to account for each until she spelled 'Christmas Past.' *Clever but not clever enough, witch!*

Her suspicion verified, her thoughts returned to Arthur and Austen. Were they alive or dead? She had witnessed Arthur's execution and heard the explosion that presumably had taken Austen and Santa's lives, but neither fact could be proven for certain using the logic of distorted time.

If Christmas Past returned Dr. Hamilton and myself to the past, four years earlier, which is now, my present, then Arthur and Austen should be alive. Just because they die in their future doesn't mean they didn't exist in the past.

Beverley wasn't sure if her reasoning was correct. It sounded secure, but who could say with Christmas Past? It would be sometime next year before she had saved enough money to start house hunting and eventually move in next to Arthur. Or would she? Would the future play out the same way the second time around? No one, not even the Ghost of Christmas Future could predict that, it was too fluid. There were as many possibilities for the future as there were decisions made on a daily basis. All she could say is that when she *did* move in next year, Arthur had told, or *would tell her*, that he had been living there for three years. She had to see for herself.

Beverley nearly injured herself hurrying to get dressed. Without thinking, she put on the same jacket she wore on her future trip to the North Pole. When she shoved her keys into the jacket pocket, she felt a stack of cards and pulled them out. There in front of her eyes were Christmas Present's notes written in Claire's hand. *'My name is Christmas Present. I am the Ghost of Christmas Present.'*

Why had these survived her trip through time, she wondered? Was it because they were not natural to her world and belonged in the North Pole? The questions were far beyond her ability to answer; nonetheless, she was grateful for their presence in confirming her memory.

Beverley quickly thumbed through the stack, appended with a variety of multi-colored post-it notes, stopping whenever she saw Arthur or Austen's name. When she turned the stack over, she found her name spelled in bold letters, underlined and followed with three exclamation marks. *Do you spell Beverley 'L-Y' or 'L-E-Y'?*

"L-E-Y," she happily reminisced and ran out the door to confront her future.

CHAPTER 34

With traffic at a minimum, Beverley sped across the bridge toward the quiet historic peninsula and its complicated maze of narrow one-way streets. Many of the traffic lights had already reset to flashing yellow caution lights allowing her to reach her destination with relative ease.

She turned onto Carolina Place and slowed as she neared her future address, looking at the houses along the way and noting any change. Ahead of her, an ambulance with its lights flashing was parked, blocking the street just beyond her future driveway. She pulled over, shut the engine and walked the rest of the way.

Nosy neighbors standing on their porches whispered conspiratorially as EMT's loaded a gurney into the back of the ambulance. Beverley waited under the shadow of a large oak tree to see whom it was or from what home they had emerged. Herbert McQueen, a trusted fixture in the neighborhood and self-declared 'Westside Mayor' stood watching silently with his hands in his pockets. Beverley approached, careful not to mention that she knew him and inquired about the victim.

"That was Arthur's wife they took out of there on that stretcher," he said pointing to the duplex.

"What happened to her?" asked Beverley.

"I don't know," he said with obvious concern, then added, "Hope it ain't nothing' serious, but then again, ambulance here. That can't be too good."

Both watched in silence as one EMT climbed in the back as the other shut the door preparing to leave. A frantic Arthur exited the front door carrying a child in his arms and leaped into his car as the ambulance raced off. He hurriedly backed out of the driveway, barely missing the fence, but not the curb, and then burned rubber to catch up. Beverley raced to her car and followed him. She assumed that they were headed the closest hospital, the Medical University, only a few blocks to the south.

Beverley pulled into visitors' parking just as Arthur was entering the emergency room carrying Austen. Arthur had never spoken to her of the circumstances surrounding his wife's death, and she never dared ask because it was none of her business. That memory belonged to he and Austen. However, now that she sat in the car watching the events unfold in front of her, she wondered what actually happened and more importantly, wondered if she went in, what would happen. *Will this part of the past play out the same if I become involved?*

A pang of guilt cut through her as the memory of Arthur's words shortly before he met his end resounded in her head. His 'I love you' and her subsequent kiss followed later with her silently mouthing 'I love you' in return made her feel as though she were carrying on an illicit affair with a man she had yet to meet.

What if she went in and Camille did meet her end this night, would Beverley still move in next to Arthur next year? If she did, could she live with herself knowing that for the next three years she would have to relive the past through future eyes and look at Austen and Arthur nearly every day knowing what awaited them in their future? It was all too confusing and painful to think about. A teardrop landed on her forearm, informing her that she was crying.

Beverley sat in her car for the next 30 minutes trying to make sense of it all. During that time, she had come to a single conclusion rather quickly. Regardless of Camille's fate, she would not move in next to Arthur the following year. She had spent the remaining time trying to understand the ramifications of her decision. If she chose to live elsewhere, the future would change, but to what extent? Would Christmas Past still develop the formula in the future or had she taken it into the past with her and was already manufacturing the fragrance? That reality sounded the most reasonable, but if it were so, then it wouldn't matter where she lived. Mankind's future was already set on a course of assured destruction. However, if that were true, there would be no need to involve Arthur or Austen in any future plot since she already had what she wanted.

Then there was the matter of Santa Claus. Was he alive? If so, at some point, whether now or in the future, Christmas Past would have to find a way to get rid of him if she were to execute her plans. She had Arthur's recorded confession, but if he were to be her patsy, he too would need to die in order for her to justify the future coup.

The only recourse Beverley had was to warn Santa, if he were still alive that is. Assuming he was, she would need to gather as much information as possible about the players involved. Beverley took solace in one fact; neither Arthur nor Austen knew whom she was. With her anonymity intact, she exited the car and slowly walked through the doors of the Emergency Room.

"Can I help you?" asked a nurse.

"Yes, I'm looking for the Fishers. They just came in here."

"Are you a member of the immediate family?"

"Yes," Beverley lied. "I'm her sister."

"She's in observation room 115," she replied, pointing the way.

"Thank you."

Beverley followed the signs and slowed at the sight of Austen seated on a bench in the wide hallway. A few doors beyond her, nurses and attendants hurriedly entered and exited a room Beverley assumed was 115.

Her suspicions proved accurate when Arthur stepped outside and stood in the doorway with a look of concern on his face. Austen stood up and took a few steps to join him, but he quickly intercepted, picked her up and whispered some words in her ear as he walked her back towards the bench.

From Beverley's vantage point, she could see the tremendous effort he was making to present a calm face to his worried child. He kissed Austen gently, set her down on the bench then motioned her to stay put as he hurried back to his post outside Camille's door.

Beverley couldn't help herself. She walked over and took a seat next to Austen. Arthur looked at Beverley briefly, and seeing compassion registered on her face, sighed gratefully for any unsolicited help.

"Hello," said Beverley in an upbeat tone.

"Hi,' returned Austen sadly. "Are you here to see my mommy?"

"Yes."

"She's sick," offered Austen immediately as children are prone to do.

"Well, the doctors here are really, really good. They'll take good care of her." Beverley felt guilty reassuring the child, but what else could she do? "I'm sure she'll be fine."

Arthur stiffened when the doctor exited the room and escorted him a few feet away. Though his back was turned, Beverley could tell by his body language and the doctor's apologetic manner, that Camille had passed away. Not wanting Austen to see her father struggling to cope with the traumatic news, Beverley did her best to keep up the small talk.

Beverley spied as the doctor squeezed Arthur's shoulder then left him to deal with his loss. His shoulders went limp as he wiped away tears before slowly turning and making his way toward them. Beverley took the cue to leave and excused herself by bidding Austen goodbye.

Standing at a distance, but still within earshot, Beverley watched with admiration Arthur's ability to compose himself for the sake of his child. He took a knee and looked into Austen's optimistic eyes. In the three years she would have known him in the future, she had never seen this side of the man and felt ashamed that she had ever doubted it existed.

"Is mommy gonna be all right?" asked Austen.

He didn't answer her right away. Instead, he stalled by straightening her clothes, then hugged her and gently laid her head on his shoulder to hide his face before answering.

It was not easy to hide tragedy from a child. Once discovered, their undeveloped minds lacked the ability to process the event. Unless it was handled with care and sensitivity, they tended to blame themselves and carry the emotional scar with them throughout their lives, sometimes resulting in the gravest of injuries to themselves, if not others.

"Yeah, sweetheart, mommy's going to be fine." He fought to sound normal as tears streaked down his face behind her back.

"Can I see her?" Austen asked hopefully.

He quickly wiped his eyes as Austen raised her head to see his response.

"No, not right now, honey. She's . . . sleeping. The doctor doesn't want anyone to disturb her right now. She needs to rest. Okay?"

"Okay. Will she be coming home for Christmas?" asked Austen.

"Don't worry honey . . . she'll be there with us. She'll always be there with us."

The response was a tender and loving lie not meant to deceive or escape responsibility, but issued out of love and a desire to protect his child. His bravery astonished Beverley and made her wonder if she possessed such strength. Overhearing him brought to mind the night they would sit in front of her fireplace and the question she would ask him. *'What's wrong with letting Austen believe in Santa Claus? She's going to find out soon enough he isn't real, why do you have to tell her? What's the harm?'*

Now that she was privy to a perspective previously unknown, Beverley finally grasped the meaning behind his response, *'I don't like lying to her.'*

"C'mon sweetie, let's go home, you must be tired."

Beverley dipped her head as the teary-eyed Arthur walked past her toward the exit. She turned to look at Austen, her head on his shoulder, and waved a weak farewell. Austen managed a flickering smile and waved back with her fingers.

As they stepped through the doors into night, the combination of Beverley's feelings for both of them, along with the painful memory of their potential future set in motion by the tragic event she had just witnessed, overwhelmed her emotions. She staggered to the bench still warm from Austen's touch, broke down and openly cried.

The nurse she had encountered earlier saw her crying and offered her condolences. "I'm sorry for your loss."

"What happened?" sobbed Beverley.

"The doctor said it was an aneurism. There was nothing they could do."

The nurse sat with her for a few moments, and then offered her condolences once more before leaving.

In a final act of farewell, Beverley decided to drive past the Fisher house on her way home. She parked across the street and silently offered a prayer to a family she knew and loved even though they did not know her. The light was still on in Austen's bedroom, and she wondered what Arthur was saying to Austen. Moments later, the light went dark.

Beverley caught herself smiling at the irony. Her future side of the duplex was vacant, illuminated by a single porch light. Because of his hurried exit and time spent at the hospital, Arthur's side remained brightly lit, and the only home on the street whose Christmas lights were still on.

She waited there until he switched them off, and finally understood why he refused to decorate his home for Christmas.

Armed with a pad of paper, Beverley sat in front of her fireplace and began to compose her first letter to Santa Claus since she was a child. Over the next hour, she detailed everything that had happened and was going to happen. Along with her letter, she included the article on the lottery winner and Christmas Present's note cards.

After sealing it, she addressed the manila envelope with Santa's actual address, then thought better of it and simply wrote, 'Santa Claus – North Pole'. Remembering Austen's letter, she penned 'For Santa's Eyes Only' and 'Urgent Review' on both sides in bold letters. Satisfied that she was doing all she could, she curled into a ball in front of the fireplace and drifted off to sleep.

COLIN QUASHIE

EPILOGUE

"I will honor Christmas in my heart, and try to keep it all the year. I will live in the Past, the Present and the Future. The Spirits of all Three shall strive within me. I will not shut out the lessons that they teach," said Ebenezer Scrooge.

'A Christmas Carol' - Charles Dickens

CHAPTER 35

Beverley ushered Arthur into the living room with her hands covering his eyes. "Don't open them until I tell you." She released her hands then tiptoed into position with her camera poised to take his picture.

"Okay, you can open your eyes now."

The flash temporarily blinded him. As soon as the sunbursts cleared, he saw that he was standing in front an incredible Christmas tree.

"It's beautiful! Thank you!"

"This is not just any Christmas tree," informed Christmas Present. "It's an eternal Christmas Pine grown only in our forests. It never dies. After Christmas, wrap it in a sheet and stow it in a cool dark place. Each Christmas, set it up, give it some cool water and in no time, it regenerates and grows these fragrant, cinnamon scented cones." He plucked one and handed it to Beverley. "Take a whiff of that."

"Uhmmm, that smells wonderful," said Beverley savoring the sweet scent. "This is so cool! I want one."

"Where's Austen?" asked Arthur. "I want her to see this."

"She's upstairs with Santa," replied Christmas Present.

The mood upstairs was not as jovial as the one shared below. Santa sat on the edge of the bed next to a melancholy Austen staring into her hands. The silence between them was thick with disappointment and the air rife with apology. In an effort to break the stalemate, Santa reached into his bag and handed her a small gift.

"Here. That's a little something special, from me to you."

"Thank you," she replied courteously, raising her head long enough to flash him a polite smile. She held the gift in her hands, rolled it over slightly, then placed it beside her before defaulting to her original position.

"Aren't you going to open it?"

"Yes . . . later."

Santa lazily dragged his hat from his head, toyed with it briefly, and then stared into it as though there were notes written inside. The pain on his face was palpable. He had dedicated his life to making children happy, yet it seemed he had little to offer the one child to whom he owed everything.

Austen's persistence over the years had set in motion a chain of events that had eventually led to the unearthing of Christmas Past's conspiracy, but not before it had taken his life, hers and Arthur's.

Because of the depth of Beverley's love for them and her promise to remember, he was alerted to the plot in advance, but had allowed it to play itself out in order to identify all of the participants. Moments before the sleigh was to explode a second time, the crew had been evacuated and carried to safety in his original wooden sleigh powered by the reindeer. To complete the ruse, the sleigh was operated remotely by Mission Control and allowed to explode as security forces rounded up the conspirators without incident. At the same time, he and Austen made a scheduled appearance in the courtyard and stopped the execution by crushing the diminutive general under the heel of his boot before it could give the order to 'fire'.

Knowing that his decision had made Austen relive the most difficult part of her young existence over again, even though she was unaware of her repeated past, weighed heavily on his mind.

"Austen, I've been delivering gifts for . . . a very long time and I have never received a request quite like yours before. There are people that will tell you I can do a great many things. Most of them I can, as for the rest . . . I simply do the best I can. But this gift, this thing you wish for . . . it is beyond my power to give."

He paused for any response or sign of comprehension, but she remained as stoic as ever. He reached out and took her hand in his. He could feel her pain and fought for some way to get through to her.

"I understand," she finally said.

"You really miss your mother, don't you?"

She nodded sadly. "I didn't get a chance to say good-bye and tell her I loved her."

Her confession was heartbreaking. For three years, she had written him, and each time he had agonized over her request before having it filed 'undeliverable'. He had taken comfort in the fact that she would grow older and wiser, and like all human children, would eventually modify her concept of Santa

Claus from a literal fact into a figurative belief. He had no doubt that she would forgive him and chalk her childhood request up to the innocence of youth. He was also sure that in the coming years she would have found a way to honor her mother's love and treasure what little time they had had together.

He lifted her onto his lap, picked up his present and handed it to her. "Open it."

Austen unwrapped the gift slowly. She eased open the lid and drew in her breath at the sight of a cameo with Camille's portrait delicately carved in relief on the surface of the layered gem. She held the box closer and slowly ran her finger over the delicate oval. Santa removed it and hung it around her neck.

"Do you really believe in the true spirit of Christmas?"

"Yes."

"You're not just saying that to make me happy, are you?"

"No. I believe."

"Then take this cameo," he said, placing it carefully in the palm of her hands, "and cup your hands like this." He gently squeezed her palms together around the portrait.

"Now close your eyes and think of your mother."

Austen did as he instructed. She closed her eyes tight and brought the cupped treasure close to her face.

"Reach out for her," whispered Santa. "Search the darkness for the light that was her life and listen for her voice. Feel for her presence. Remember what she looked like, what she smelled like, how it felt when she held you, kissed you, and told you how much she loved you. Call out to her with your heart and find her."

"Mommy," whispered Austen. He could tell by her furrowed brow and the sight of her eyes darting back and forth under her eyelids that her desire to see her mother was stronger than her unanswered loss.

"Yes, that's it," encouraged Santa. "Keep thinking of her and how much you love her."

Austen wasn't sure what she was seeing. Initially, she was scared by the self imposed darkness, but soon afterwards, her eyes adjusted and the veil of blackness began to part into cloudlike shades slowly taking form, drifting nearer then disappearing as puffs of light blossomed, giving dimension to the gloom. The more she concentrated, the more she saw until a fuzzy aura of mist began to coalesce and condense.

Santa waited with anticipation for what seemed forever to a man who truly understood the term. Suddenly, he felt her body shift, indicating the vision was near. Her wrinkled brow released and rose with astonishment.

"I see her," whispered Austen. "I see her."

"Then open your eyes and look."

Austen slowly opened her eyes and saw a wispy glow hovering before her. A vision tried to form, but soon faded.

"You must believe, Austen. You must believe! Concentrate," he urged.

She closed her eyes tighter and cupped the cameo hard with added effort. The fading glow immediately brightened.

"Yes, that's it . . . that's it."

As the form began to take shape, he gently tapped her cupped hands, signaling her to once again open her eyes and behold the image hovering in front of her.

The vision of a baby crying in a crib, greeted her. It squirmed beneath the quilt folded across her bed. Mesmerized, she slid from Santa's lap and stood before it.

"That's me," she whispered. "Where's my mommy?"

"I'm coming, sweetheart," answered Camille entering the vision.

"Mommy, mommy, it's me," cried Austen. She reached out to touch the dream but Santa's gentle hand on her shoulder advised otherwise.

"She can't hear you. She is but a vision of what was, brought here by your love for her."

"Oh sweetheart, what's wrong? Don't cry, mommy's here," comforted Camille.

Austen's eyes moistened with tears as she watched her mother pick her up, cradled her to her breast and take a seat in the rocking chair located on the far side of Austen's bed. As she slowly rocked, the crying subsided until silence filled the room. Moments later, she began to quietly sing to her child.

> *Silent night, Holy night,*
> *All is calm, all is bright.*
> *Round yon Virgin, mother and child,*
> *Holy infant, so tender and mild,*
> *Sleep in heavenly peace,*
> *Sleep in heavenly peace.*

By the time Camille had finished, the child was sleeping. Austen watched as Camille eased from the rocking chair, placed her in the crib, covered her with the quilt, then kissed a finger and touched it to her forehead.

Camille stood there watching Austen, then slowly backed away. She was about to exit, but suddenly stopped, turned and looked around the room as though she had heard a familiar, though faint voice and was searching for its source.

Austen edged closer as Camille scanned the room until her gaze settled. She seemed to peer directly at Austen through the portal of mind as though able to see her in a vision of her own. Austen's desire drew the living portrait of Camille closer until her translucent face hovered close enough for Austen to touch.

It was the moment Austen had waited for. For three years she had wondered what she would say and how she would feel, and now that the moment was here, she knowingly realized that the volume of words she had imagined uttering could never describe the longing or the love that existed between mother and daughter.

"I love you."

Camille's face filled with and pride as she mouthed, "I love you," in return, then kissed her finger and extended it toward Austen who did the same.

The imagined touch, though only an emotional expression of their real love for each other, satisfied both completely. Camille raised her hand to wave goodbye, and then knowingly pulled it away, as if a promise to Austen that she would always be there for her and as an invitation to return.

The vision soon faded. Austen turned to Santa with tears streaming down her face.

"Bring her back! Please, bring her back!" begged Austen.

"I can't. Only you can do that," replied Santa hugging her to his chest.

"How?"

"The same way you brought her here." Santa lifted her onto his lap and reached for her cameo.

"This is a special gift made just for you. Whenever you want to see your mother, find a secret place, close your eyes, and hold it tightly like I showed you. As long as you love her and truly believe, it will always be filled with happy memories of you and your mother for you to cherish forever."

It had taken Santa two years to make. He could easily have had one of his many artisans craft the gift in a fraction of the time, but instead, he had sat in his old workshop and worked night after night, painstakingly carving and polishing it to perfection. Once completed, he mounted it in a silver setting of his design and attached a chain created link by link. After that, he had summoned all of the magic and mystery the North Pole had to offer and imbued the gift with its hidden power.

"Now, listen to me." He shifted her around on his lap and stared directly into her eyes to underscore his warning. "Don't lose this. It's the only one of its kind. It belongs to you and you alone. And whatever you do, don't tell anyone, not even your dad or Beverley, about its power or it will fade. Do you understand?"

"Yes," she said with startling gravity.

"It'll be our secret, okay?"

"Okay."

"Come on. We better get downstairs. They're waiting for us." He wiped her face and smiled as she stared at the cameo, then slid it under her shirt. She reached for his neck and hugged him tight, then thanked him and hugged him once again.

"No, Austen . . . thank you."

Santa escorted Austen downstairs and joined everyone in the foyer.

"Present, I think it's about time we leave these people to enjoy their Christmas."

"Santa, Christmas Present . . . I don't know how to thank you for everything you've done," said Arthur.

"Don't thank me, thank her," corrected Santa and nodded in Beverley's direction.

"Don't worry," said Arthur. He gave her a loving look and reached for her hand. "I will."

"Oh, before I go, I have a little something for you," said Santa. He reached into his bag and handed Arthur a gift. Arthur pulled off the bow then handed it to Beverley to finish opening. She ripped it open and laughed at the contents. It was a Christmas tree ornament. Frozen inside the clear glass globe were two figurines of Christmas Past and Christmas Future standing in the courtyard.

Arthur held the ornament close and stared into the life like face of Christmas Past. "Right where she belongs."

"Can I hang it on the tree?" asked Austen.

"You sure can, little lady," said Beverley.

Everyone smiled as Austen took the ornament and darted into the living room.

"Well Present, time for us to leave. You remember how to get back?"

"How could I possibly forget?"

"You're not letting him drive, are you," asked Beverley with feigned concern.

"It's quite alright. Since a certain someone whose name I won't mention has no use for her memory anymore, Santa gave it me."

"Congratulations!"

"Thank you, Beverley. B-E-V-E-R-L-E-Y. Beverley."

She laughed at their little joke and gave him a hug.

Arthur and Beverley held hands and waved goodbye as they began to fade, then reappear a moment later.

"I almost forgot," said Santa. He pointed toward the ceiling and a branch of mistletoe mysteriously appeared. He winked at them and with a wave, faded away with Christmas Present.

"You know," said Arthur staring playfully at the mistletoe. "I had a strange dream last night that seemed so real, and you were in it."

"I was," said Beverley edging closer.

"Yep. I was tied to a candy cane pole and was saying something to you about embarrassing myself . . . but I can't remember how it ended."

"I can," said Beverley and kissed him hard.

Santa knew exactly what he wanted to give Austen for Christmas, but had to think long and hard about what to give Beverley and Arthur. It finally occurred to him that what they both wanted and needed most wasn't something from him, but from each other.

Beverley had changed her mind and made the painful decision to move in next to Arthur and Austen the following year. She had agonized daily over their future, afraid to warn them lest she alter their future, and by extension, mankind's. She had placed her hope and trust in Santa, and he had rewarded her long suffering by giving back to Arthur and Austen their past memories of the time they had spent with Beverley. For both it was if no time had passed.

Austen ran back in the foyer and caught them kissing under the mistletoe. Happy to finally see them together, she hugged both.

Arthur held Austen's hand and stepped away from Beverley. "We have something for you."

Austen pulled a small gift box from her pocket and handed it to Arthur, who in turn presented it to Beverley. Surprised by their thoughtfulness, she ripped it open and froze. Arthur took the ring from the box and as rehearsed, both sank to one knee.

"Beverley Tynes, after all we've been through, together and apart, will you marry me?"

For the first time since he known her, Beverley was speechless. She swallowed hard trying to hold back tears and looked into both of their eyes.

"Only if Austen will have me as her step-mother."

The smile on Arthur's face and Austin's tight hug around her waist answered her question. The new family held each other in a loving embrace for the next few minutes, well within sight of the solitary ornament hanging on the magical Christmas tree, containing the Ghost of Christmas Past and Christmas Future . . . frozen together in time for all eternity . . .

THE END?

ACKNOWLEDGEMENTS

A sincere debt of gratitude is owed to Christine Castaneda for patiently editing the manuscript and mentoring a first time writer. Thank you to Kathryn Gailey and Preston Lancaster for their careful eyes and notes. Vincent Williams, your contagious inspiration and continued words of encouragement are a blessing. Thanks to Orlando Jones who apparently sees more in me than I do. Tony Bell, thanks for always having my back. Your friendship is a rock.

C. D. Q.